HEROES OF MUSIC

TITLES IN THE HEROES SERIES

Heroes of the American Indian
Heroes of Israel
Heroes of Mexico
Heroes of Science
Heroines of America
Heroes of Conservation
Heroes of Puerto Rico
Heroes de Puerto Rico
  (Spanish language edition)

Heroes of Journalism
Heroes of Music
Heroes of Peace
Heroes of Nature

ABOUT THE AUTHOR

Renée B. Fisher has written extensively on music for various periodicals and served as music critic and radio commentator. She is a member of the music department of the University of Bridgeport. Previously, she taught music at Brooklyn College, Long Island University, Southern Connecticut State College, and in the public school systems of New York City and Westport, Connecticut. In addition to playing the piano and doublebass professionally, she has conducted vocal groups and composed music for various media.

HEROES OF MUSIC

by

Renée Fisher

FLEET PRESS CORPORATION
New York

© Copyright 1974, Fleet Press Corporation
160 Fifth Avenue
New York City 10010

Library of Congress Catalogue Card No.: 79-161375

ISBN 0-8303-01 01-1

*Quotation from GEORGE GERSHWIN: HIS JOURNEY
TO GREATNESS, by David Ewen, © Copyright,
1970, Prentice Hall, Inc.*

contents

HEROES OF MUSIC

music

What It Means To Us
How It All Began
Its Heroes, Known and Unknown

What would our lives be like without music? Missing would be the sheer wonder of how sounds can be put together in so many wonderful ways—bright, dark, smooth, choppy, loud, soft, quick, slow, high, low, tinkling, growling, calm, excited—and of how those sounds can bring about so many varieties of emotion and enjoyment.

People hum when they are happy, lull babies to sleep with music, console themselves by singing or playing an instrument, play a recording to mirror their moods. One twist of a dial provides the right background for doing homework, or ice-skating, or helping to release many kinds of emotions. Without music there would be no parades; football half-times would be less spectacular, movies less moving, holidays less memorable, parties less cheerful. There would be no dancing, either socially or on the stage. Religious services would be less uplifting, weddings less gay, funerals less meaningful. Life itself would be poorer in so many ways.

No one knows for certain just how and when music

9

originated. There have been many fascinating guesses. Some think it may have grown out of speech sounds. But there were many other sounds in definite patterns around primitive man— the steady patter of rain on his cave, the regular beats of his own pulse, the steady rhythm of waves on the shore, and the various bird calls. Men and women for thousands of years must have tried to imitate these sounds by stamping their feet, clapping hands, yelling, rattling sea-shells or animal bones. Eventually, instead of imitating natural sounds, some unknown hero (perhaps a number of them in different parts of the world) hit on a combination of sounds that seemed pleasant or useful to him. He tried playing or singing it again. Although he didn't realize it, he was making music—for all of music is organized sound.

Music was a vital necessity, as well as a pleasure to primitive man. There are people in remote parts of the world who live today in much the same way that their ancestors did thousands of years ago. They give us valuable clues to the role of music in primitive society. Certain music scholars who have devoted their lives to studying these communities feel that music was of even greater importance in primitive times than in our own.

Consider communications, for example. Even today the famous "talking drums" of the Yoruba tribe in Nigeria still carry messages across jungle distances, using complex rhythms that require great musicianship on the part of the drummer. There are work songs that men created to help them pull oars together, or to haul rope with a steady beat. Or a shepherd learned that certain tones sung or played soothed his flock and kept them together. There is even a Somalian song to encourage camels to drink water.

Music was often considered a form of magic and an important part of religious ritual. Since it was felt that music could subdue the forces of nature and also ward off misfortune and bad "spirits," the finest singer often became the priest because of his "magic" musical ability. There are songs of prayer for a successful hunt, songs and dances to instill courage in the hunters, musical prayers for their safety, and musical
10

celebrations upon their safe return. There are invocations by musician-priests for rain and good crops, and against famine and plagues.

All the important events of life were celebrated with special music—birth, adolescence, marriage, death, harvest, war. Among the Sioux Indians, for example, every young man in the tribe had to learn to play the flute; his playing of a certain song to the girl of his choice was his proposal of marriage. Among various American Indian tribes there can also be found children's songs, dream songs, songs for curing illnesses, dance and game songs, personal narratives, songs honoring individual heroes, and songs imitating the movements and cries of animals.

What about instruments? There is much speculation but little proof of how instruments were invented. No names have come down to us of the thousands of people over the centuries who brought the guitar, for example, to its present form. But we can trace its beginnings clear back to the vibrating twang of a hunter's bow. Someone had the brilliant idea of bending the bow permanently and attaching several strings of animal gut across it. That was the first crude harp, from which all plucked string instruments, including the guitar, are descended. In the course of many years ingenious experimenters found that by mounting strings on a box-like wooden frame they could get greater resonance. That revolutionary discovery led gradually to the shape and tone-quality of our modern violin, guitar, autoharp, etc. A piano, too, is actually a kind of harp, even though the strings are struck with hammers instead of being plucked by hand or pick.

Perhaps the best-known name in the perfecting of instruments is Stradivarius. Antonio Stradivarius and two of his sons made violins in the seventeenth and eighteenth centuries. These were instruments of such beauty and rich strong tone that kings, princes, composers and performers from all over Europe came to the little town of Cremona, Italy, to order his violins. They were, and are today, considered to be the most perfect ever made. His methods of construction, the shape, size and curves, are still used for the finest violins made today. But even now no

11

one is able to duplicate the original master. It is not known what the elusive secret was—whether it was some particular source of the wood Stradivarius used or the way he "cured" it or, more likely, the brilliant transparent varnish with which he finished each instrument.

What of the drum? In forest areas man soon discovered that the resonance of a hollowed-out tree trunk with an animal skin stretched across it was much greater than clapping hands or stamping feet; played by hand or stick, those were the first drums. Man used whatever materials he found around him. He clicked sea-shells together. In Hawaii a hollowed-out gourd is used as a drum, and highly polished stones are hit against each other for a brilliant, clacking sound.

Once man learned to work metal many new instrument possibilities arose. The sound of metal on metal led to bells, to the vibraharp and the triangle. One family, the Zildjians, devised a formula for making cymbals of exceptional quality. Today's Zildjian cymbals are still produced by that closely-guarded secret formula. But Stradivarius and Zildjian are exceptions. Very few of the heroes of instrument construction are widely known.

What about the blown instruments? Flutes and other wind instruments began in areas where there was reed to be blown into or bamboo into which holes could be carved. It was a long series of inventive steps from that point to the intricate fingering devices of our modern clarinets and bassoons, to say nothing of the addition of a keyboard to reeds to make the accordion, or the adding of pipes to make an organ. Only one man was lucky enough to have his name attached to an instrument that he helped to perfect—Adolphe Sax, whose name is immortalized by the saxophone.

As for the bugle, trumpet, trombone, horn, etc., their ancestors were the horns of domestic animals and those killed in hunting. The trombone acquired its slide in medieval times, but the valves which added to the very few natural horn notes were invented less than two hundred years ago. The "shofar" or ram's horn blown in all synagogues today at the beginning of the

12

Jewish New Year is identical with the one used in Biblical times.

The Bible is one of the most important sources of our information about music in ancient times. It is true that some fragments of actual ancient instruments have been discovered; clay tablets and cave drawings have also been found which show people singing and playing instruments. The Old Testament, however, gives us detailed references to the role of music in people's lives at the time. There was dancing and singing before the temple ark in praise of God. It is evident from the psalms that a leader sang one line, the congregation responding with the next, and many different instruments are named and described. There must have been fine players of the lyre (a type of harp). The young David was selected by representatives of King Saul from among many contestants to soothe the old King's spirits by playing at his court. Later David established a network of schools to train musicians. There may have been as many as four thousand men (women were excluded) taking part in the services in the main temple.

What about today? Are instruments still being invented now? They are. Most of them are electronic. Not only have existing instruments such as the guitar and bass been electrified, but completely new instruments in which the original sound is produced electronically are now being used. The "Synthesizer," by R. J. Moog, for example, can produce sounds of any tone-quality, loudness and speed desired; it can imitate the sound of the human voice or any instrument, and can be made to produce totally new sounds. Computers have been built that can be programmed to produce music unlike any music ever heard before. These are very difficult to learn to use. Many colleges have computer laboratories in their music departments to train composer-engineers for the future.

Even without elaborate machines of this kind many new effects are possible through electronics by manipulating tape recorders: speeding up sound, slowing it down, or superimposing one tape on another. Many of these new effects are used in popular music today. Interestingly enough, while some popular musicians are exploring these new frontiers of sound, there are also some who are reviving the use of older, traditional

13

instruments from all parts of the world. The banjo, traditional folk instrument of early America, is very popular once again. The Beatles, a few years ago, stimulated interest in the music of India when they introduced the Indian string instrument, the sitar, in some of their recordings.

There have been fashions in instruments—they have ups and downs in popularity. Sometimes it takes just one great performer to revive interest in an old instrument. About sixty years ago Wanda Landowska became fascinated by the harpsichord, ancestor of the piano. By her magnificent performances in concerts and through recordings she aroused world interest in the instrument. Now over a hundred companies are making harpsichords to keep up with the demand. It is used in jazz as well as classical music.

Unfortunately we cannot tell how early music sounded. Music notation had not yet been devised. It is unfortunate that from the ancient Greeks, who left us magnificent samples of their sculpture, architecture and literature, there are only a few fragments of music, though they considered music to be one of the greatest arts. It is only in recent years that music scholars have been able to translate the notation of those fragments, so that they can be played and heard today.

Up to the twelfth century (except for the Greeks) it was not possible to capture sounds on paper. There was no special language of music. Music was learned by the "oral tradition," that is, it was learned by heart from other performers, just as most folk music was and still is learned. More complicated music could not be memorized easily. At first, monks trying to preserve the music of religious services of the Middle Ages, used a type of shorthand—signs put over the words to remind the singers of what to do next. It took many anonymous heroes several hundreds years to invent the system of musical notation we use today—and even today it is far from perfect. Many of the rhythms used in jazz, for example, cannot be written exactly as they are meant to be played. Neither can folk music which uses any sounds other than the semitones of our notational system.

We can look at paintings or read books ourselves, but

music, obviously, does not exist until it is performed and heard. There have been great heroes of performance who have been able to reproduce whatever composers wrote for them. By their superb singing or playing they often stimulated composers to be more daring and inventive in their compositions.

It is the composer-heroes who concern us here, for without them the shape, the direction, the qualities of Western music as we know it would be entirely different. There are so many that only those who made the greatest impact on the history of our music can be covered. We start a little over four hundred years ago with the composer who first pointed his art in the direction that led to the music of today.

claudio monteverdi
1567-1643

Monteverdi sat at his desk in the Court Chapel in Mantua, Italy, torn between what he had to do and what he wanted to do. Strewn about him were music for a new ballet, schedules of rehearsals with singers and players for a concert, scenery and costume designs for a musical *intermezzo* to be performed between the acts of a new play, musical programs to be planned for a reception, feast and ball in honor of a visiting prince. In addition, the regular musical church service for Sunday had to be rehearsed and performed as usual.

The year was 1605. Artusi, the learned monk and writer on music, had been attacking him in print for five years, claiming that Monteverdi was corrupting the pure art of music as it had been practiced for centuries. Each attack angered him anew. "Your new rules are distorted and unnatural . . . alien to the purpose of the artist, which is to give pleasure. The harshness of your discords stands out . . . as though intended to agonize the ear."

What if the Duke of Mantua became convinced Artusi was correct? It was only Monteverdi's reputation as one of the most accomplished and talented composers of the day that assured him his position at the Court. His life was not easy. Overworked and underpaid, he barely made enough to support his wife and two sons. He had had to plead for the job to begin with. "I humbly apply to become director of music in your chamber and chapel. If your goodness and graciousness make me worthy of it I shall receive it with that humility becoming a modest servant when he is favoured and gratified by a great prince such as Your Highness . . ." In later years he remembered bitterly how payment of his tiny salary was often delayed. He wrote to a friend: "I did not suffer any greater mental humiliation than those times when I had to wait in the antechamber to obtain what was due to me."

The Duke loved to display his wealth by elaborate musical and theatrical events, but he depleted his treasury with the upkeep of a magnificent palace and gardens, and by adding to his collections of Chinese art, tapestries and tulips. The musicians, artists and poets on his staff were at the bottom of the list financially, and socially as well.

If only, Claudio thought, he could sweep all these projects off his desk, and write a blistering book in reply to Artusi. But the Duke must be served. His music would have to speak for him.

What did Artusi really object to? The musical practice of the two hundred years before him was thought to be perfect and at its height when Monteverdi introduced his innovations. The "Renaissance," meaning "re-birth," had been a time of exploration of the world, of the arts, of the possibilities of man. The soaring magnificence of its architecture, the vibrant colors of its artists, the expansion of science, inventions and commerce, were reflected in music too. Folk songs, those sung by the common people, usually consisted of a single line of melody notes with or without accompaniments. The Renaissance composers, who worked largely for the church or the nobility, had gradually added other melodic strands to the original religious chants, interweaving them with great skill and later with strict rules, into a style called "polyphony," meaning many-voiced.

17

There was a large body of magnificent music for Monteverdi to build on. Giovanni da Palestrina (1524-1594) had been the greatest sixteenth-century composer of religious polyphonic music and had also written beautiful secular works for several voices (these were called *madrigals*). Orlandus Lassus (1530-1594), a Flemish composer, had brought a new strength and magnificence to madrigal-writing as well as sacred works. Some of the madrigals and solo songs of William Byrd (1543-1623), an English composer, foreshadowed in many respects Monteverdi's writing in those forms.

But in the hands of less gifted composers polyphony became so complicated and so full of musical tricks that it lost all contact with the words and their meaning. Monteverdi sensed that this musical style was dying, that the future lay in an entirely different direction. He was a master of the older technique, as he demonstrated in his many fine madrigals; he wrote most of his religious music in the conservative Renaissance style, but he did not really believe in it. He felt that the wave of the future in music should be similar to what was happening in the other arts—that it should be not only as impressive as the new architecture, as ornamental and vital as the sculpture, but also as expressive of the individual, his feelings and emotions, as the new poetry. He wrote, "I very well realize that our feelings are mostly stirred by contrasts, and that to arouse emotions of the heart and soul is the aim of all good music."

How, then, to handle Artusi? Monteverdi's younger brother Giulio was a fine musician who assisted with the music chores at Mantua. He volunteered to write a brief statement for inclusion in the next collection of his brother's music to be published. It would show that Monteverdi not only knew all the old rules, but that every time he broke them it was for a good musical reason. Giulio explained that the new approach tried to "make the words the mistress of the music, and not its servant." Claudio was most grateful to his devoted brother for coming to his defense in this way, but still felt strongly that telling his musical ideas was not enough. He longed for an opportunity to show through a new major musical work his revolutionary ideas.

18

That opportunity came about two years later at carnival time. A few years before, a group of poets and musicians, trying to capture what they imagined to be the spirit of ancient Greece, conceived the idea of setting a play completely to music, thus inventing what we call "opera." It was a daring blend of poetry, singing, instruments, acting and dancing in one new art form. The Duke of Mantua had seen one of these early spectacles at Florence and seized upon opera as a perfect vehicle for displaying his princely power. The solo singing gave him an excuse to hire singers with the most beautiful voices; the elaborate costuming and magical stage-effects such as cloud machines would bring new glamor to his Court, and he had Monteverdi, an infinitely better composer than the earlier experimenters in opera, to provide the music.

The result was *Orfeo,* based, like all early opera, on an old Greek myth. It was the first great opera, performed many times during Monteverdi's lifetime, and is the earliest opera still performed today all over the world.

Orfeo gave full play to the composer's new ideas about writing for instruments as well as for voices. Until then, because the Church had frowned on the use of instruments, composers were mostly voice-oriented. When they wrote instrumental music they did not specify exactly which instruments were to be played. Since composers usually conducted their own music they simply used whatever instrumentalists were available to them. If another composer's music was played, whichever instruments could play the range of the required notes were assigned to the parts. Monteverdi changed that. He listed every instrument by name at the beginning of *Orfeo* and chose each one carefully for its particular effect. The trombone, for example, helped create the atmosphere of hell, and the flutes quiet pastoral scenes. Even though the orchestra was hidden behind the stage to concentrate attention on the singers and action, Monteverdi's careful underlining of every scene with instruments that exactly expressed the mood made the orchestra an important element in opera from that time on.

His handling of the vocal elements was superb. Even in the

19

short time that opera had been in existence singers were already trying to dominate it, using the composer's notes as taking-off points for added brilliant ornamental notes that would show off their voices. Monteverdi kept the singers in check by writing all the ornaments exactly as he wanted them sung, leaving no opportunity for singers to put themselves, rather than the music, first. The star singers were delighted with their roles, for never before had they been given the opportunity to sing such expressive music. The music required their highest acting powers to match the intensity of the music's emotions. The words and music were blended into a single overwhelming experience.

Orfeo brought Monteverdi more fame than any other composer of his times. The year of its production, however, brought with it great personal grief as well as new triumphs. Monteverdi's young wife Claudia died unexpectedly, leaving him with two young sons. He had hardly recovered at his father's home from this tragedy when he was summoned urgently back to Mantua for an elaborate series of festivities. For his son's forthcoming marriage, the Duke ordered a new theater to be built. Monteverdi was in charge of all musical performances connected with the wedding—an opera, a ballet and a comedy. They had to be written, rehearsed and performed in so short a time that the composer could never recall, without shuddering, those few months of his life when he thought he would collapse from overwork.

The opera, *Arianna,* was his crowning achievement. A contemporary of Monteverdi's described the first production, "The brilliance of the production was so spectacular as to amaze all present . . ." As many as six thousand were reported to be present.

Almost all of this opera, unfortunately, has been lost, with the exception of its most famous song, the "Lament of Arianna." Perhaps its deep, touching melancholy was an outpouring of Monteverdi's recent personal grief. One spectator wrote: "The Lament of Arianna, abandoned by Theseus, was sung with so much warmth and feeling and represented in so moving a manner that all the listeners were most profoundly stirred and

20

Claudio Monteverdi

none of the ladies remained without tears." The men must have succumbed too, for another report says, "He composed the aria (song) in so exquisite manner that it visibly moved the whole audience to tears." The "Lament" became known quickly throughout Europe, and was admired by composers, poets and audiences. No opera during the rest of the century was complete without a lament, and even thirty years later every musical household had a copy of Monteverdi's song. It was called "the most beautiful composition of our time." Monteverdi was now famous throughout Europe, overshadowing composers of his own day, and in his final triumph over Artusi, over the composers of the Renaissance.

Shortly after this musical triumph the Duchy of Mantua began to decline from the impact of a series of disasters which included deaths, intrigues, war and the sacking of ducal treasures. But Monteverdi's personal star continued to rise. When he resigned he left Mantua almost as penniless as he had entered it. But the begging was now on the other side—the rulers of Venice pleaded with him to accept a post which was the ultimate ambition of every famous musician, that of musical director of the Cathedral of St. Mark. He was given a hero's reception there, a good salary, an apartment, sole charge of thirty singers and twenty players, and the opportunity to accept commissions from princes and other churches. He even occasionally accepted commissions from the new Duke of Mantua, with the delightful difference that he could now refuse them when he was too busy.

How he loved Venice! Physically it was considered the most beautiful city of the time. The Cathedral where Monteverdi worked was a wonder to behold. Centuries of conquest had brought innumerable treasures to decorate it. The capture and looting of Constantinople added Oriental domes, bronze horses, gold, crystal and enameled objects and tapestries. The finest artists and sculptors for several hundred years had spent their lives fashioning works of art for the walls and ceilings. The clothing of the nobility matched their surroundings in elegance. Their chief occupations were attending masked balls, concerts, pageants, festivals and private entertainments. Magnificent religious processions were held in the ornate mosaic-tiled plaza in front of the Cathedral.

But it was more than the physical beauty that made the city so dear to Monteverdi. To him it spelled freedom, splendor, honor, personal comfort, gaiety and opportunity for all his talents. Not only were there gala banquets for important state visitors, but many private evening musicales were held at palaces by the music-loving noble families of the city. Indeed, few musical events went on in Venice without him.

Most of the religious music and operas Monteverdi wrote in Venice have been lost. Fortunately however, his very last opera, written at age seventy-four, two years before his death, has survived. The youthful vitality and imagination displayed in this work, *The Coronation of Poppea*, were amazing for a man of his age, as were the many new and revolutionary innovations it included. He streamlined the orchestra, ridding it of many of the less flexible instruments. He used a much smaller orchestra than the one for *Orfeo*, and made the string instruments the most numerous. In this he laid the foundation for the modern orchestra, which still centers on the strings and uses the other instruments for change of color and special effect. He also made great demands on the violinists, forcing them to extend their range to notes higher than they had ever played before. He introduced the idea of laying aside the bow and plucking the notes with the fingers—an unheard-of effect called *pizzicato* which became standard after that. He was also the first to suggest agitated speech by having a note repeated rapidly many times in succession *(tremolo)*. It is hard to imagine how music of the eighteenth and nineteenth century would have sounded without these innovations.

Even his subject-matter was daring. In *Poppea* he discarded the Greek myths for real history, thus paving the way for operas of the future, based on people experiencing genuine emotions, rather than on remote, heroic characters in unreal situations. The singing was intensely emotional, the arias connected by a song-speech *(declamation)* which heightened the meaning of every word. The characters kept their in-

23

dividuality—each one had a musical tag for identification. A certain set of notes played by the orchestra or sung signaled the arrival of a particular person, and mirrored his personality.

Monteverdi founded a completely new operatic style which took possession of all Italy, and then Europe. However, for various reasons his life and work were in oblivion for almost two hundred years, until some of his music was rediscovered during the last century. It took the twentieth century to appreciate and recognize his genius. Every revival of his operas, with their astonishing musical richness and their love and feeling for life, convinces a new group of listeners that he truly deserves the title "Father of Modern Music."

johann sebastian bach

1685-1750

If a vote were taken among trained musicians today to find out whom they considered the single most important figure in the history of music there is little doubt it would be Johann Sebastian Bach. His life was unspectacular; he never left the small central German province of Thuringia in all of his sixty-five years. One of the more unusual aspects of his life was the size of his family—he fathered twenty children (nine of whom survived him).

He was born into a family that had been musicians for at least four generations before him. Every Bach boy was expected to go into music. Almost every town in Thuringia had a Bach as its church organist, choirleader or town musician. As a young child Johann looked forward to the annual reunions of the family, when all the Bachs gathered to exchange news and to make music together.

His parents were both dead by the time he was ten, and a brother with whom he then lived, himself a church musician, gave Johann a good musical education on the violin, organ and "klavier" (as all the other keyboard instruments of the time were called). Even at this early age, Johann showed an overpowering curiosity about all music and an eagerness to play everything he heard.

He must have been a very bright student in general, for we know that he was only fourteen in a class of eighteen-year-olds at the local academy. By fifteen, when his scholarship ran out, he was sent to a monastery school which offered poor boys with good voices permanent places in its choir. Here Johann became acquainted at first hand with the rich fabric of polyphonic choral works of the greatest masters of the past centuries. His abilities were soon recognized, for when his beautiful soprano voice changed he was kept on as violinist and organist.

His curiosity took him repeatedly to Hamburg, famous for its organs and its tradition of great organists. He visited a nearby academy for young aristocrats, where he learned the French style of composing instrumental music. He thought nothing of traveling fifty or sixty miles on foot to hear French music at the provincial court of Celle, or to any Thuringian town that boasted a fine organ or outstanding organist. By intensive listening, copying down what he heard, and trying the music for himself, he made every current idiom part of himself.

The Bach family grapevine probably helped him get his first church position, the first of many. There are letters, petitions and contracts that help us understand why he changed jobs so often. As *cantor* of a church he usually was involved in extensive teaching and training of the choirs and orchestras under him. He was a superb teacher of composition, klavier and organ on a one-to-one basis, but had little patience with a roomful of unruly choirboys, only a few of whom had enough interest and ability to meet his demands. A musical perfectionist, Bach quarreled bitterly with church authorities about the poor human material at his disposal. He had arguments over his salary and his overburdened schedules. One censure of him (when he was twenty-one) asks, "By what right he recently caused the strange maiden to be invited into the choir loft and let her make music there?" The "strange maiden" may have been Maria Barbara, his first wife, whom he married the following year, but her

26

identity has never been proved.

Much later, in Weimar, the authorities went so far as to imprison Bach for "too stubbornly forcing the issue of his dismissal . . ." He finally was freed from arrest with notice of his unfavorable discharge. His move to Leipzig was made largely to provide his children with better educational opportunities. He had been in Leipzig for seven years when he outlined some of his complaints in a letter to a friend: "(1) The position is not nearly so advantageous as I had believed. (2) Many of the incidental fees have been withdrawn. (Funeral fees, he indicated, were much lower than he had expected because the healthful Leipzig climate reduced the number of funerals!) (3) The town is very expensive to live in. (4) The authorities are queer folk, little devoted to music, so that I have to endure almost constant annoyance, vexation, and persecution." He then asked his friend to let him know of any possibility of a better position. Obviously nothing better turned up, for Bach spent the remaining twenty years of his life in Leipzig.

Much as he was dissatisfied with his working conditions most of his life, Bach the composer evidently thrived on it. Through it all he managed to turn out the required new music week after week for the church service plus special large pieces of music for town events, as well as instrumental music ordered by the local nobility for performance at Court. He wrote the music, rehearsed, and often accompanied or conducted the actual performance.

His musical output was astonishing, especially since he also was regarded as the outstanding organist (in an age of great organ-playing) of Europe. Not only did he compose and play organ music which was considered impossibly difficult, but he was also recognized as an authority on the instrument itself. Hardly an organ in all of central Germany was ever accepted until "old Bach" had tested it thoroughly and played an inaugural recital on it.

He was a deeply religious man who dedicated each of his works "to the glory of God." If the body of his religious music is remarkable, no less so is his secular music. Both of his wives were musicians, as were most of their children. The house rang with music from morning to night, with Bach teaching his wife and children, and the whole family frequently making music together. His second wife, Anna Magdalena, was herself a fine musician. Both for her and for his several musically-talented children Bach showed infinite patience. Some of his greatest keyboard works are those he wrote as "exercises" to teach Anna Magdalena or their sons Wilhelm and Johann Christoph some technical point. Far from being considered dull exercises, his *Well-Tempered Klavier* has been the Bible of pianists ever since.

He had the great satisfaction of seeing several of his sons continue the Bach tradition by becoming outstanding professional musicians, two of them with much more financial and social success than their father. The one who most closely identified himself with his father's style was the eldest, Wilhelm Friedemann Bach (1710-1784) who, inheriting his father's originality, wrote strong works for organ and piano, and became one of the great organists of his time. The second son, Carl Philipp Emanuel Bach (1714-1788) and the youngest, Johann Christian Bach (1735-1782) belonged to a new breed of composers who gradually abandoned polyphonic music as "old-fashioned."

Most of Bach's music gathered dust for almost a century, except for a few composers who recognized its value and were deeply influenced by it. A full revival of interest in Bach's music did not occur until about 1830, eighty years after his death.

The musical, economic and personal reasons that impelled Bach to change his positions were troublesome from his point of view. But these periodic changes of circumstance, hard as they were on Bach, were his music's gain. His first two positions were periods of apprenticeship. Already rich in ideas and imagination, Bach did not yet have the technical maturity that came later. These early years as a church musician, until he was twenty-three, were times of experimentation and of imitation of all the music he had ever heard or learned about. The pattern of his creative life was set early—he was employed as a performer and composer. His works belonged to his employer and were written to meet the specific needs of a church or private per-

28

formance. His earliest church cantatas, which were sacred concertos for solo voices and various instruments, as well as numerous klavier pieces, were written in this early period. But most impressive were his brilliant, fanciful organ works such as the *Toccata and Fugue in D Minor* and the *Little Fugue in G Minor*. Both his organ works and church cantatas were grounded in patterns laid down by an earlier German composer, Dietrich Buxtehude (1637-1707), but very early Bach's genius put a stamp of originality on the old forms.

When Bach, at twenty-three, was appointed Court organist and chamber musician to the Duke of Weimar, he continued writing religious music for the Court Chapel, and rose to unprecedented heights as an organist. He extended organ technique by creating new fingerings, including extensive use of the neglected thumb, which made faster passages playable. In the words of a contemporary, "he was able to accomplish passages on the pedals with his feet which would have given trouble to the five fingers of many a klavier player on the keyboard."

No other instrument is indebted so heavily to one composer for its music and its performance as the organ is to Bach. For it he wrote chorale preludes, which were imaginative variations on familiar Lutheran hymns such as *A Mighty Fortress Is Our God*. Besides numerous original works such as the *Passacaglia in C Minor* he also arranged violin and keyboard works, by himself and by other composers, for the organ. He managed, in his magnificent and dramatic organ output, to use that instrument's full capacity for effective contrasts and tingling climaxes of sound, adding his brilliant originality to all that Italian music and the German organ tradition had previously attained. Also at Weimar Bach continued to write church cantatas, in which he combined the sacred concerto with some elements of Italian opera in his own inimitable way. He also wrote works for keyboard instruments and sonatas for string and wind instruments.

But the greatest flowering of Bach's secular music came during his six years at the court of Prince Leopold at Cöthen. The Prince loved chamber music and hired highly skilled in-

Johann Sebastian Bach

strumentalists, thus stimulating Bach's genius in new directions. It was here that he wrote the six *Brandenburg Concertos* for orchestra, with their flowing melodies, expressive slow movements, exuberance, and sense of drama as well as logic. If he had written nothing else, Bach would still be a supreme master for the grandeur and magnificence of the suites and sonatas for the violin, and also for cello. We still marvel at how he was able to suggest polyphonic and harmonic sounds on instruments that could produce no more than two notes simultaneously. Bach wrote for many instrumental combinations, but particularly important are the klavier works he wrote to help him in teaching his wife and children. Among them were the *Inventions* (some of which were written by little Wilhelm Bach), the French Suites and English Suites, which were sets of dances, the *Little Klavier Books* and the first part of the *Well-Tempered Klavier,* that most cherished of all keyboard works.

If Cöthen gave Bach little scope for religious composition, there was plenty of such opportunity in Leipzig, where he served for the last twenty-seven years of his life as cantor and musical director of St. Thomas's Church, the heart of the German Lutheran movement. He was responsibile for the music in four churches, musical instruction for the choirboys in the church school, as well as his own family and outside pupils. Bach was inspired here to heights of composition in every direction except opera, which he had no occasion to write.

He composed some secular cantatas such as the *Coffee Cantata* and *Peasant Cantata,* a set of klavier suites, some organ works and the second part of the *Well-Tempered Klavier.* He also wrote the *Italian Concerto* and the *Goldberg Variations*—two great works for the harpsichord. With these he changed the role of the harpsichord from that of a musical maid-of-all-work to that of a solo instrument. But the Leipzig period is immortal above all for his vocal church compositions. Among perhaps two hundred and fifty church cantatas of this period *Sleepers Awake* is particularly well-known. *The St. Matthew Passion,* with its simplicity and directness and rich accompaniments, is thought to be among the most moving and wonderful of all examples of Protestant music. But greatest of all was the monumental *Mass in B Minor*, set to parts of the Catholic liturgy, but too immense in its scope, length and musical requirements to be an actual part of any religious service. If one musical work were to be named as the greatest expression of religious exaltation this Mass, which took twenty-five years to complete, would be it.

What made Bach such a great hero? As with many of the heroes of music, he did not invent any new musical forms of writing or new instruments. He did carry almost all of the existing forms to new heights, and reveal possibilities for giving old instruments utterly new, startling roles both technically and expressively. It is through his compositions themselves that Bach shows himself to be the greatest musical figure of the day. Known as the Baroque period, it was a time when artists, architects, poets and composers were intoxicated with the wealth of material at their disposal; when buildings were more magnificent, colors more flamboyant, words used more extravagantly than ever before. In their search for more expressive depths many succumbed to exaggeration of ornament, whether in architecture or music, thus sometimes marring the end-result as a work of art. There was a "rightness" about Bach's musical instincts which kept him from that fatal error.

Bach undoubtedly knew of, and drew inspiration from, the delightful and charming keyboard works of William Byrd (c.1543-1623) the great composer of keyboard music who also invented the theme and variation form. He also studied very carefully the organ and harpsichord works of the French composer Francois Couperin (1668-1733) and the Italian, Domenico Scarlatti (1685-1757). Their influence is evident in Bach's dance suites. Two Italian composers, Arcangelo Corelli (1653-1713) and Antonio Vivaldi (1675-1741) helped shape Bach's thinking in his solo sonatas, solo concertos and concertos for orchestra.

A true son of the Baroque, Bach "thought big." His smaller works are usually part of a larger whole with a magnificent master plan which fits the smaller pieces into place with

32

beautiful proportions. His melodies are expressive, his harmonies forceful and rich. His rhythms are full of vitality and subtle variety, with an underlying feeling of continual flow which gives a sense of unity. Above all, he was a master of polyphony. He had the gift for creating entirely contrasting and independent themes that could go together in remarkable ways. He then developed them with and against each other in such complex and exciting ways that musicians today are awed at his mastery.

He not only fused polyphony and harmony into one, but he also unified the whole concept of different media. This he did by applying keyboard idioms to string music, violinistic ideas to klavier music, etc. He wrote instrumental music that sounds vocal, and vocal music that seems instrumental. There have been many heroes of music; few indeed are the others who ever reached the level achieved by Bach.

george frideric handel

1685-1759

Handel was born in the same year as Bach with only forty miles separating them. They were both Lutheran, both were supreme virtuosi of the harpsichord and organ and masters of polyphony, and both became blind in later life. Yet they never met, and their seemingly parallel beginnings led to utterly different lives. Bach's family expected him to become a musician; Handel became one over the strenuous objections of his non-musical family. Bach never left Thuringia; Handel was a well-traveled man of the world who eventually became a British citizen. Bach's habitat was the provincial court and church, his cronies the local fellow-musicians; Handel was equally at home in the salons of the nobility and the business offices of the many opera companies he managed. Bach's life was a series of small vexations, everyday problems and minor triumphs; Handel's ventures, both successes and failures, were on a grand scale.

Bach enjoyed an intense and rewarding family life; Handel remained a bachelor. Bach wrote in nearly every idiom except opera; Handel made his great reputation mainly through opera.

34

Bach was buried humbly, without fanfare or acclaim. His reputation awaited artistic resurrection many years later. Handel was buried with great pomp in Westminster Abbey, but somehow has never regained the level of popularity he enjoyed during his life, and never approached Bach in the musical esteem of later generations. Yet their careers were each typical of the Baroque period in which they lived.

Handel's father, sixty years old when George was born, hated music passionately, and allowed no instrument within the walls of his home. A respected barber-surgeon, he performed some nearly-miraculous cures which earned him a visiting consultant's status at the nearby Court of the Duke of Weissenfels, in addition to his local practice. Fortunately for George, their town of Halle was a very musical one. He had only to walk about town to hear various civic bands and street musicians, or wander into the numerous churches to hear fine choirs and organists practicing and performing.

Somehow the boy must have persuaded some organist to show him the rudiments of that instrument. He was no more than seven or eight when he accompanied his father on a visit to the Duke's court. No less a person than the Duke himself happened accidentally to hear young George improvising on the Court chapel organ. The Duke at once ordered the father to take immediate steps to have the boy, with his obvious talent, trained in music. What a blow for the old man, who looked upon music as the work of the devil and musicians as little better than street beggars! He could not possibly refuse to carry out an order by his most influential patron. Thus Handel was launched on the most intensive three years of his life. Those years turned out to be the only formal music training he ever received.

Fortunately Zachau, the local organist who taught him, was a fine, accomplished musician and composer. Handel learned composition and organ of course, but also oboe, harpsichord and violin. During those three years he wrote more than a hundred church services as well as instrumental pieces (very little of this music has survived). At the end of the three years, Zachau declared that he had taught his pupil all he knew. About the time he was eleven George visited Berlin, where the Elector Friedrich III and his musical wife Sophie were so taken with his performance on the organ and harpsichord that they wrote to Handel's father, offering to send his son to Italy for advanced training. His father, now on his deathbed, refused absolutely. After his father's death Handel's mother carried out her husband's wishes by insisting that Handel study law. Music was a magnet, however, that continued to draw him throughout his school career. He continued to write music, organized a student chorus to perform his works, and filled in for the leading church organist who had been dismissed. He began to draw the attention of all visiting musicians, including Georg Telemann (1681-1767),—the only composer besides Handel whose name eventually became a household word in eighteenth-century Europe.

By eighteen George started out for Hamburg, leaving home and the study of the law. He had no trouble finding work there in an orchestra, and he now had the leisure and opportunity to absorb theater, opera and concerts. He soon struck up friendships with established and rising composers such as Reinhard Keiser (1674-1739) and Johann Mattheson (1681-1764). Before long he was not only teaching, but had also been commissioned to write a religious work and an opera. He now had sufficient money and reputation to fulfill what he felt to be his destiny—a visit to Italy, cradle of music.

He made his mark there quickly. In Rome his good looks, letters of introduction and talent earned him this recognition: "There has arrived in this city a Saxon, an excellent player and composer of music, who has today displayed his ability in playing the organ in the Church of St. John Lateran to the amazement of everyone." There was an edict at that time which forbade performances of opera in Rome itself, so Handel threw himself into religious composition. He secretly worked on his first Italian opera and found the audiences of Florence and Venice wonderfully encouraging. He made friends easily, this time acquiring Domenico Scarlatti of the famous Scarlatti

36

musical family as a traveling companion. Through him, as well as several cardinals and princes who appreciated his talents, Handel managed to live by his musical wits until his first full-scale triumph. The opera *Agrippina,* which he wrote in three weeks was received enthusiastically and performed twenty-seven times. It was also during this Italian visit that he became acquainted with the works of Arcangelo Corelli, famous violinist and composer who undoubtedly exerted a strong influence on both Handel and Bach in their sonatas for solo instruments and orchestral concertos.

With this Italian triumph behind him he returned to Germany. Handel became chapel master at the Court of Hanover, earning more at age twenty-five than Bach earned at fifty. Financially perhaps he was satisfied, but his sense of musical adventure did not let him rest. Almost immediately he asked for leave to visit London, known then as a wicked and fascinating city. Without a single word of English or friend to turn to, Handel still managed in the space of a year to write and produce the opera *Rinaldo,* which catapulted him to instant fame. But Hanover still had claims on him and he returned there, writing chamber music and songs for the Court, studying English, and determined to return to England. When he left Germany at twenty-seven it was forever.

London fascinated him. It was a large, sprawling, cosmopolitan city that attracted many cultured foreigners, and took its pleasures very seriously. Among these were the theater, music, elegant dress and witty, malicious gossip. Opera, with its opportunity to show taste in singers as well as clothes, ranked high on the pleasure list. There was no composer in all England that could match Handel, and his operatic successes soon made him the darling of all London society. A birthday ode he wrote for Queen Anne earned him a comfortable pension and enabled him to go on with his opera ventures, organ recitals and musicales in private homes of the nobility.

By a peculiar coincidence of musical and political history his old patron in Germany, the Elector of Hanover, became

King George I, following his former chapel-master to England. Handel soon worked himself back into royal favor. His good relations with the King are amply borne out by the story of one of Handel's finest orchestral compositions, written superbly for outdoor performance, the *Water Music*. An account of its first performance records: "On Wednesday evening the King took water at Whitehall in an open barge and went up the river towards Chelsea. Many other barges with persons of quality attended . . . a city company's barge was employed for the music, wherein were fifty instruments which played all the way the finest symphonies, composed expressly for this occasion by Mr. Handel: which His Majesty likes so well that he caused it to be played over three times in going and returning."

For the next forty years Handel spent most of his time in daring what few composers before him had done: to woo the public through the box-office. Opera in the Italian style was the fashion. The stories were fairly improbable, many based on ancient myths, and had little action. They were spectacular in costuming and stage-setting, but the singers hardly pretended to act. Most spectacular of all were the voices. The singers underwent rigorous training which gave them a range of notes, breath control and a virtuoso style that amazed the audiences. Composers wrote for the particular singers in their opera companies. The *da capo* aria had been perfected by the Italian composer Alessandro Scarlatti (1660-1725). It was a song in which the main theme was stated, then a second, contrasting section introduced, after which the main theme was restated. When the main theme returned, the singer was given freedom to invent his or her own embellishments and ornaments to best show the voice's capabilities. What happened between the arias was simply a kind of half-spoken, half-sung musical conversation to carry the plot forward and connect aria to aria. There were occasional choruses for massed voices, but the opera was subordinate to the role of the star singers.

Handel threw himself into the world of opera, writing almost sixty in the course of his life, sometimes acting as producer as well as composer. His self-confident, stocky figure

38

was well-known all over England and the Continent. He had to coax wealthy people into backing his operas and search the opera houses of Europe to get the best singers. He learned to negotiate with wealthy merchants, influential nobility, temperamental singers and demanding stagehands and musicians.

There were many hazards for this businessman-composer to face. Other composers, such as Giovanni Bononcini (1660-1750) and Johann Hasse (1699-1783), tried to challenge his supremacy by staging their own operas in rival opera houses while Handel's were being performed. Sometimes he had to write a new opera in such a short time that he borrowed melodies from other composers or from himself, adapting them to his immediate needs. This practice was not frowned upon then as much as it would be now. Coping with the often vain and greedy desires of some of the favorite singers and their supporters often drove the short-tempered Handel into a rage.

In the twenty years that Italian opera held sway in London Handel made and lost a fortune several times, always maintaining enough resiliency to bounce back. He hated to stop writing opera even when the demand finally began to wane. London eventually grew tired of performances in Italian, a language it did not understand, and when *The Beggar's Opera* by John Pepusch (1667-1752) was produced in 1728 it spelled the doom of Italian opera. It not only was in English, but it spoofed everything about Italian opera and used simple, sturdy English tunes that the audience could hum.

Handel, ever resourceful, found a new area for his talents. His reputation had never rested entirely on opera. His concertos, chamber music and organ works were a familiar part of the musical scene in private homes and public gatherings throughout England. As official music master to the royal family he was called on to submit music for special occasions, such as the autumn festivities for the coronation of George II. Among the new works Handel wrote for the occasion was *Esther,* to be performed in the Royal Chapel. It was so successful that it was repeated in a commercial theater. It was originally written for a semi-religious observance and performed without acting. This

George Frideric Handel

started Handel on his second career—as composer of oratorios.

An oratorio is a part-opera, part-concert performance without action, based on plots taken from the Testaments, with great use of chorus. The English loved it. They knew the stories, which Handel found to be much more exciting than the old opera plots. They found the choral parts to be overwhelming in their grandeur as sung with the support of a large orchestra. All of England went so "oratorio-mad" that the new style crowded out every other form of music. It was many years after Handel's death before English composers were able to throw off the weight of his influence on their writing.

There is no question that Handel, as well as Bach, drew inspiration for their choral works from the earlier German composer Heinrich Schütz (1585-1672), who introduced monophony and also double choruses into German religious music. His mingling of the new Italian emphasis on solo singing with the old German polyphonic choral tradition resulted in a more expressive dramatic style which found its culmination in Handel's oratorios. And it is by his oratorios rather than his operas that Handel is best remembered today. Among those most performed are *The Messiah, Judas Maccabeus, Israel in Egypt, Samson,* and *Saul.* When his most famous oratorio, *The Messiah,* was first performed, so many tickets were sold that the newspapers asked ladies to come without hoops in their dresses, and gentlemen without their swords, so as to increase the audience capacity. It was during the first presentation of *The Messiah* in London the following year that the famous *Hallelujah Chorus* incident occurred. As an eyewitness described it: "When Handel's *Messiah* was first performed, the audience was exceedingly struck and affected by the music in general, but when the chorus struck up "For the Lord God Omnipotent" in the *Hallelujah,* they were so transported that they, together with the King, started up and remained standing till the chorus ended." From that day to this, audiences have stood up during the singing of the *Hallelujah Chorus.*

The Messiah was very profitable for Handel. He donated most of the proceeds to his favorite charity, the Foundling

41

Hospital, of which he was governor. His triumphs in oratorio led to a commission to compose music for the "Royal Fireworks" celebration of a recently-signed peace treaty.

It was while working on the oratorio *Jephtha* that Handel first realized he was losing his sight; a painful operation did not help. He continued composing and playing even after becoming blind. He dictated new music and gave organ recitals throughout the nine years of his blindness. We can imagine how greatly moved the audiences must have been when a singer standing beside the blind composer at the organ sang the aria from *Samson,* "Total eclipse! No sun, no moon! All dark amid the blaze of noon."

When he died in 1759 he was mourned throughout England and the Continent as a great man as well as composer. In the years after his death his works were tampered with, and the orchestras and choruses performing them enlarged. By the time of the Handel festivals in London in the late 1800's about five thousand musicians took part.

The importance of the oratorios was realized all along. It is only lately that his operas, too, are being produced and recorded with the care they deserve. The musical values of Handel's music are hard if not impossible to define. The traits that made him a great man made his music great—it is strong, direct, self-confident music. Handel was a keen observer of the musical scene, having thoroughly absorbed all that was best in German, English, Italian and French music. He used these various idioms in his own writing with a sure instinct for what was most appropriate in any given situation. His keen, sympathetic understanding of people resulted in vivid musical characterizations. He had a strong sense of the drama in human relationships and was able to translate that drama into sound.

Even though Handel's music has a simple, convincing effect, his command of the art is far from simple. He favored beautifully spunout long melodic lines, sturdy rhythms, strong contrasts of speed and volume, and expert use of polyphonic texture when he felt the need. Generally his music, in contrast to Bach's, was basically homophonic, that is, having a single dominant melody with the rest of the sound subordinate to that

42

line. In keeping with his role as an outstanding composer of the Baroque period, Handel's large works are marvels of form, and they project a rich magnificence and grandeur. His musical output was even greater in quantity than Bach's, so that if only a small portion of his vocal and instrumental works is revived each year we can look forward to wonderful new musical experiences for many years to come.

franz joseph haydn
1732-1809

In the course of his seventy-seven years Franz Joseph Haydn rose from a humble, peasant-like origin to become the recognized and undisputed leader of the world of music. Surely that is not the way he envisioned his future when he was thrown out of school at eighteen to shift for himself, with nothing but three clean shirts and a worn coat as his total worldly possessions.

His musical abilities were evident when he was a child at home with his father, a wheelwright, and his mother, a former cook. He sang Austrian, Hungarian and Croatian folksongs with his father, staying in tune and keeping time with a stick, in their tiny cottage in the Austrian village of Rohrau.

When a distant cousin, Johann Franck, who was a schoolmaster and church cantor in the town of Haimburg, offered to give Joseph a chance for a good musical education, the parents realized with a pang that they had to accept for the boy's sake. At five-and-a-half Joseph left his warm and loving home forever. The Francks were kind people, but their home was poor and crowded. Joseph often went to bed hungry as well as dirty, but his sunny good nature kept him happy. The new schedule was rigorous for a six-year-old—school from seven to ten, attendance and duties at Mass, school again from twelve to three, then homework and music instruction.

Haimburg was a religious town, with many processions and festivals. Joseph had numerous opportunities to sing and otherwise put his early music lessons to good use. However, instruction in other fields was sketchy, and throughout his life Joseph felt the lack of a good education.

It was when Joseph was eight that the composer Reutter, looking around the countryside for promising choirboys for the great Viennese Cathedral of St. Stephen's, spotted his small but sweet soprano voice. He could use a voice of that purity and beauty, and Joseph was soon bundled off to the great city to live with Reutter and the other choirboys in a house next to the Cathedral. The years with his cousin must have seemed like Paradise compared with his life at St. Stephen's for the next nine years. If anything, the food was even less and of poorer quality and Reutter exploited the boys, treating them mercilessly. He trained them to be expert singers, and taught them some klavier and violin, but their practical knowledge came from their duties—two full choral services every day, special programs for feast days, private concerts, funerals, processions, outdoor programs and court appearances. The boys especially looked forward to their visits to the Court where they were served good food.

Vienna was a city full of music, and young Joseph absorbed it all. "I listened more than I studied, but I heard the finest music in all forms that was to be heard in my time, and of this there was much in Vienna. I listened attentively and tried to turn to good account what most impressed me."

Worst of all was the fact that Reutter starved the boys' minds as well as their bodies, teaching them little about musical theory or anything else. Reutter was an experienced if not an inspired composer, yet when Joseph tried to write an original piece Reutter laughed at the naive errors, and gave him no help at a time when it would have meant so much to the boy.

45

Through it all Joseph's natural good humor and high spirits kept him from self-pity. He was very happy when his younger brother joined the choir. Shortly after his brother's arrival, Joseph's voice began to change; he could no longer sing. Reutter cast about for an excuse to get rid of him, and found it in a childish practical joke. One day Joseph cut off the pigtail of one of the other choristers, thereby providing Reutter with his excuse. First beaten and then expelled, Joseph found himself penniless, at eighteen, on the streets of Vienna. In his own words, he had to "eke out a wretched existence for eight whole years" before his luck changed. He was ill-equipped as a musician, poorly dressed, unattractive, naive, without manners or friends. He wandered the streets, depending on stray acquaintances to offer him a place to sleep and a little food. Gradually, painfully, he began playing at dances and in taverns, arranging music, and taking pupils at pitifully small fees. Most of his money was earned as a "street musician," hired to play serenades outside the window of a lady on her birthday. He made the best of his cold attic, studying intensely by himself, and acquiring an "old, worm-eaten klavier."

When his voice finally settled down he was fortunate in meeting the outstanding Italian singing teacher Niccolò Porpora, then a man of seventy. In exchange for singing lessons and a little money, Joseph not only accompanied Porpora's students, but also served as a kind of valet, cleaning shoes, arranging wigs, doing domestic chores. One time, he tried desperately to get a certain choir job; the choirmaster wouldn't listen to him. Joseph stole into the choir loft, took a vocal part out of a singer's hand, and sang the solo so perfectly that "all the choir held their breath to listen." He was hired. He also occasionally had the opportunity to write some chamber music for fashionable private salons of the city. A typical day's work was usually about sixteen hours. A contemporary remembered: "At daybreak he took the part of first violin at the Church of the Fathers of the Order of Mercy; thence he repaired to the chapel of Count Haugwitz, where he played the organ; at a later hour he sang the tenor part at St. Stephen's; and last he passed a part of the night at the harpsichord."

It was shortly after Haydn was hired as music director and court composer by Count Morzin, that he made the greatest mistake of his life. Disappointed when the girl he loved turned him down (she became a nun) he married her sister, Maria, although he scarcely knew her. Older than Haydn, not attractive, unpleasant, uninterested in music and his career, she made his domestic life miserable. In later years he referred to her as "that infernal beast." To his great sorrow, they never had children.

Professionally, however, Haydn's star was finally rising. At Count Morzin's court he received a respectable sum of money plus free room and board, and had an orchestra of sixteen players at his disposal. When Count Morzin had to give up his expensive orchestra, Prince Esterhazy, a powerful Hungarian noble, remembered the delightful symphonies he had heard at the Morzin Court. He was building a palace to rival Versailles, and wanted music to match it in splendor. The name of Esterhazy is remembered today because of what four Esterhazy princes did for Haydn, from the time of his first appointment as court music director and chapel master.

Was it his many years of poverty and struggle that made the Esterhazy offer so irresistible? His salary was tripled, his surroundings glamorous, the music halls and instruments magnificent; but the contract he had to sign seemed to require almost complete servitude. His duties were staggering—twice that of any conductor today. Besides conducting the orchestra and singers in daily practice and many performances, he had to compose vast quantities of music. He also had many administrative duties—librarian, supervisor of instruments and repairs, management of all musical personnel, to name a few.

Worst of all, his duties were spelled out in such a way that he was obviously considered a servant, not a professional. Even the details of his uniform, which he had to wear at all times, were written into his contract. He had to report to the Prince for orders every morning and afternoon. He could not leave the palace grounds without permission, nor could he have his music copied for publication or performance elsewhere.

Surprisingly, Haydn and Esterhazy oberved that contract

for over thirty years. The Prince was determined that his court be a cultural center, and spared no expense in hiring the best singers and instrumentalists. Undisturbed by financial worries, isolated from the distractions of Vienna, Haydn was able to compose freely and to experiment. In his own words: "My prince was always satisfied with my works. Not only did I have the encouragement of constant approval, but as conductor of an orchestra I could make experiments . . . and be as bold as I pleased. I was cut off from the world; there was no one to confuse or torment me, and I was forced to become original."

He wrote at first not in the majestically splendid style of the Baroque, but in the *gallant style* which followed—works essentially light, playful and gay. The inspiration for many of his melodies came from the folk music he had absorbed in his youth. His nickname "Papa" came from his musicians, whose problems he handled with tact and good nature. He settled their quarrels and took responsibility for their actions with the court administrators.

If his music was easygoing and carefree, Haydn's musical requirements were not. He insisted on well-rehearsed performances and attention to every musical detail. In the theater holding four hundred there were performances every day of Italian opera or German comedy, as well as marionette performances. Haydn not only wrote the operas, but also the music for two concerts a week plus chamber music for performance in the prince's private apartment. Haydn was able to hear each composition he wrote as soon as the ink was dry.

Gradually he outgrew the limitations of the *gallant style,* and his own personality emerged in his compositions. There began to be a greater intensity of feeling; some deeper and darker moods began to appear, even a grave seriousness. He did not lose, however, his pleasure in flashes of the unexpected, little surprises and sudden changes. His early works had been described as "charming, ingratiating, engaging, naturally humorous, enticing." About the year 1772 signs appeared of what is called his "storm and stress" period, a kind of romantic crisis which made him daringly experimental, using polyphony,

Franz Joseph Haydn

gypsy folk tunes, and exotic variation in his melodies. The works exhibit at times an atmosphere of restlessness and suffering.

During the years that followed (despite the provisions of his contract) Haydn's music was copied, published and performed throughout Europe. The kings of Spain and Sweden decorated him; the French commissioned a series of symphonies; his operas were performed and admired everywhere. Unscrupulous publishers brought out the works of other composers under Haydn's name. Fame never turned his head; he remained a kind and simple man, benevolent and pious.

He had fame, a well-paid position, good health, great musical productivity. Why did Haydn nevertheless become increasingly moody and dissatisfied? One factor may have been his contact with Wolfgang Mozart. That younger genius, whom Haydn came to love and admire deeply, had such an entirely different, worldly, well-traveled background. No doubt Haydn began to feel life was passing him by. Perhaps he needed the stimulus of new surroundings and experiences to release the full force of his creative urge. Once he had signed himself proudly "Chapel Master to His Highness Prince Esterhazy, in whose service I hope to live and die." Now he wrote: "I am doomed to stay at home. It is indeed sad always to be a slave. Yet Providence decrees it so."

He stayed several more years at Esterhaza, finally achieving that blend between heart and mind, inspiration and intellect, which characterized the "classical" period of music. His musical ideas developed with a new beauty and composure. Haydn did not "invent" the symphony, or the sonata form which is an important part of the symphony, sonata, concerto and other musical forms. The symphony had developed gradually, at first by expansion of the opera overture by the French composers Jean Philippe Rameau (1683-1764) and Jean Baptiste Lully (1632-1687). Domenico Scarlatti had carried one-movement "sonatas" as well as keyboard playing to new heights. Most of all, Bach's second son, Carl Philipp Emanuel Bach developed the three-movement symphony and concerto. He solidified the sonata form as consisting of two contrasting themes to be stated, then developed by showing all their expressive possibilities, then

50

restated. All of this Haydn inherited. To it he added many improvements and refinements. One of the most important was a new unity he achieved by "thematic elaboration," in which the second theme grew out of the first, so that the whole movement developed from a single germ of melody—one which was broken down and reassembled in imaginative ways.

Haydn's freedom came suddenly when Prince Esterhazy, whom he had served for twenty-eight years, died in 1790. The new prince was not a music lover; he added money to Haydn's pension but left the composer free to do whatever he wished. For years Haydn had received invitations to Italy, France and England. An English violinist named Johann Salomon was most persuasive. Haydn, anxious to leave for England, left all his belongings behind. His friends worried about a man of fifty-eight undertaking the long and hazardous journey across Europe and the English Channel. Mozart wrote: "Oh, Papa, you have had no education for the wide world, and you speak so few languages!" To which Haydn answered serenely, "But my language is understood all over the world." And it was.

London's size, traffic and strangeness astonished Haydn. Despite the language barrier he quickly became part of the dazzling musical life, making friends with the leading musicians. His musical test came in March of 1791 when the first of his twelve new symphonies, commissioned by Salomon, was to be performed. It swept the sophisticated London audience completely off its feet, having an "electrical effect on all present . . . such a degree of enthusiasm as almost amounted to frenzy." This was a new sensation for Haydn—the recognition by an exacting audience in the world's largest capital was the encouragement his genius needed.

Far from going to his head, it inspired him to produce symphonies that far surpassed anything he had written before. It is amazing that so many and by far the greatest works of his entire life were written after he was sixty years old. Perhaps his great zest for living and continuing creative power were a result of the long, undisturbed years at Esterhaza. His two trips to England undoubtedly triggered this latent energy into action.

51

Hearing the symphonies of Bach's youngest and very successful son, Johann Christian Bach profoundly influenced his melodic expressiveness and flexibility in development of melodic ideas. A Handel festival he heard in Westminster Abbey moved him to tears. More important, it resulted directly in two of the crowning achievements of his busy old age—the oratorios, *The Creation* and *The Seasons*. But those works came later, when he voluntarily chose to give up the limelight and return to the seclusion of Esterhaza.

The years in London, of which he left three memorable journals full of his delighted reactions as both tourist and revered composer, had accomplished much. They had given him the confidence to compose freely. Acclaim came not only from the general public and the British music world but from the royal family. They tried to persuade him to settle in England. Oxford University had given him an honorary degree of Doctor of Music—a wonderful ego-builder for a man who never forgot his education-starved and penniless youth. The London trips, above all, opened his eyes to the beauties of Handel and choral music in general.

He needed peace and quiet again. He spent several years at Esterhaza working on *The Creation*. These were among the happiest years of his life. "Never was I so devout as when composing *The Creation*. I knelt down every day and prayed to God to strengthen me for my work." That masterpiece breathes the spirit of Handel, with its extraordinary intensity and its marvelous interpretation of every detail of the text. It is full of descriptions of nature—storms, lightning, thunder, rain, hail, snow. All of the animals of creation are depicted, the mammals, birds, fishes, insects—conveyed with freshness and a youthful outlook hard to believe of a man in his seventies.

Its first performance in Vienna was an "enrapturing evening; still the music sounds in my ears and in my heart"—the words of an eyewitness. He continued writing other music and amassing new honors. Much of his proceeds went to benefit poor musicians. He wrote a song which became the Austrian national anthem, and played it resolutely before his death, as Napoleon's

52

cannons could be heard near his house.

Haydn's last years found him weakened, in poor health, but happily receiving visitors. He composed and conducted up to the age of seventy-five. His basic joyfulness and optimism never left him. At the time of his death he was a very wealthy man. Friends, relatives and needy musicians were remembered in his will. At his funeral the *Requiem* by his beloved Mozart, whom he had befriended, was played.

Haydn was one of those few heroes of music who were truly valued by their contemporaries; his music did not have to wait until after his death to become a cherished part of the world musical heritage.

wolfgang amadeus mozart
1756-1791

Mozart was one of history's greatest prodigies. Whatever mysterious combination of inherited and acquired abilities produces one of these rare beings, Mozart had it.

His father, Leopold Mozart, was a professional musician, a court composer and violinist with a small income. He was intelligent, cautious, precise and well-organized. It was from his mother that Wolfgang inherited his sunny disposition, sense of humor, a happy-go-lucky carefree attitude towards life and a strong appetite for all of life's pleasures. He was a very striking, handsome youngster—bright, eager, affectionate, obedient, yet full of playful jokes and pranks. Little "Wolferl" and his older sister "Nannerl" lived in Salzburg, Austria.

When Nannerl was seven her father began teaching her piano. Wolferl, who was three, couldn't resist trying to play her pieces, picking out the right notes by ear. The father began to teach him also. He learned in a day what should have taken weeks, showing abnormal concentration at the piano. From then on, even his games involved music.

He had heard music and talk of music all of his young life, both at home and at court functions where he listened behind the scenes. He must have heard many a concerto (a work for a soloist accompanied by an orchestra). One day when he was four a musician friend came home with his father to find Wolferl engrossed, with quill pen in hand, writing notes on music manuscript paper. His father asked to see what he was doing. "I am writing a concerto for the klavier and it will soon be done." Amused, the two musicians looked at the paper. What they saw brought tears to their eyes. Astounded, the father sighed, "The child has not only written a concerto, but one so difficult that nobody can possibly play it." Wolferl cried out: "You're right, Papa! One must practice it until it is perfect!" He went to the klavier, reaching those few notes that his pudgy fingers could, to give his father an idea of how he meant it to sound.

One day a few months later a court violinist brought some new trios to try out. Wolferl had a tiny violin of his own but had never taken a lesson on it. He begged to be allowed to join in, saying "You do not need lessons to play the second fiddle part." Finally Leopold let him play along with the musician playing that part. Before long the grown-up stopped, letting Wolferl go on alone. They went through all six trios before giving way to their excitement, smothering the child with kisses and exclamations of wonder.

The father recognized very early that he had a composing prodigy in his son. It was when Wolferl was five that Leopold started writing down the pieces he composed, and also began teaching the boy to write them carefully and neatly by himself. As simple and childlike as the ideas were, they already showed the kind of perfect treatment that later came to be called "Mozartean."

Leopold was determined to enhance his name and his fortune through his son's seemingly miraculous gifts. Nowadays we condemn what he did as "child exploitation." In the eighteenth century it was a common and accepted practice to exhibit unusual children in their early years. People were enthralled at the spectacle and willing to pay considerable sums to see them perform. Leopold also felt that his plans would ensure

Wolferl's future. How else could even the most talented musician and composer get a desirable top position at one of the great courts if he did not build his fame early? With Wolferl's talents and his careful guidance, the son could attain the glory and wealth which had always eluded the father. How could Leopold anticipate that this ambition would wreck his son's life and lead to his pitifully early death?

He laid his plans carefully for the children, who idolized him. Nannerl too was a gifted pianist. Leopold first planned a short trip to Munich with both children, then a longer one to Vienna. Proving himself to be a first-rate publicity man, he managed to get invitations to play in salons of wealthy families and at the palaces of all the provincial nobility along their route. The children astonished every audience. Word of the new musical sensation sped ahead of them. By the time they reached Vienna every countess and princess wanted them to ornament their salons.

Finally the most important invitation of all arrived—to play for the Empress Maria Therese at her palace. That first visit to her private rooms lasted three hours and was a great success. In the course of it, Wolfgang climbed on the Empress's lap, hugged her, romped with the little princess Marie Antoinette, and announced his intention of marrying her. They spent a hectic month in Vienna, with Wolferl wearing the state costume of lilac and gold satin which the Empress had ordered made for him. One of his letters home reads: "Today we are at the French Ambassador's, and tomorrow we go to Count Harrach's. We are everywhere fetched and set home in the carriages of the nobility . . . On one occasion we were at a place from half-past two until near four o'clock; then Count Hardegg sent his carriage for us, which took us at full gallop to the house of a lady where we stayed till half-past five; afterward we were with Count Kaunitz till near nine."

The inevitable illness that followed upon this unnatural schedule for two young children forced an end to it. Wolferl contracted scarlet fever which left him weakened. The great fear of this infectious disease put an end to all further ap-

Mozart with his father, Leopold and sister, Nannerl

pearances. The trip home was typical of all the long, unhealthy journeys the children undertook during the next several years. As they traveled in unsanitary coaches over crude roads, staying in the cold, filthy inns of the day, Leopold constantly planned new ways to squeeze money out of the next town. On one occasion the press notice read "The little girl, who is in her twelfth year, will play the most difficult compositions of the greatest masters; the boy, who is not yet seven, will perform on the harpsichord; he will also play a concerto for the violin, and will accompany symphonies on the klavier, the keyboard being covered with a cloth, with as much facility as if he could see the keys. He will instantly name all notes played at a distance, whether singly or in chords, on the klavier or any other instrument, glass, bell or clock. He will finally, both on the harpsichord and the organ, improvise as long as may be desired and in any key. Each person pays half-a-thaler. Tickets may be had at the Golden Lion."

That was during their third trip, which was planned to cover all the summer courts between Salzburg and Paris. Leopold had written to every potential patron on the way. At Heidelberg, after Wolferl played an hour on the church organ, the Dean of the church, overcome, ordered an inscription carved on the organ case giving the name, age and date of the tiny player's appearance. He felt he had witnessed a modern miracle. The Emperor Francis I called Wolferl a "little magician." In Paris he played for the royal court, and also wrote his first two sets of piano and violin sonatas, which he dedicated to the king's daughter. The title page read "by J. G. Wolfgang Mozart of Salzburg, seven years old." Leopold had the children keep diaries in the language of every country they visited.

After Paris, they extended their trip to London, playing repeatedly for King George III and his court. Wolferl wrote his first symphony (Eb, K.16) on a quiet afternoon when his father was ill. He made Nannerl sit next to him to "remind me that I give the horns plenty to do." It was during this trip that Wolferl met Johann Christian Bach, Johann Sebastian's youngest son and an extremely popular figure in London music circles.

58

Mozart later acknowledged that he was profoundly influenced by him in the writing of operas. Considering it a privilege, many British musicians refused to accept fees when playing with Wolferl.

Some British music scholars would not believe that Wolferl was as young as he was advertised to be. They checked his birth records and submitted him to extraordinary musical tests, finally admitting that he was, indeed, a "prodigy of nature." By the time they reached Holland, both children collapsed from exhaustion. What did they have to show, back in Salzburg, for their trip of three years? Leopold wrote to his wife, "We could open a shop with all the presents, jewelry, swords and laces, snuffboxes, etc., that they showered on the children." But of hard cash, it was found that almost all had been spent on traveling expenses, keeping up appearances, hiring halls, etc. But the greatest cost had been in health. Wolferl, now ten, remained short and delicate all his life, not having the stamina in later life to fight the disease which killed him at thirty-five.

The next few years were spent at home in Salzburg. Wolferl studied polyphony seriously, and wrote an opera in Italian when he was twelve. In trying to get it produced he came upon an enemy that was to plague him always—jealousy. The music community recognized the threat to their reputations if a boy of twelve could compete with them by producing a creditable opera. They lined up solidly with the Italian court music director to see that the opera was not produced. The Emperor finally awarded Wolferl a minor position—an empty title—which gave him a chance to write some commissioned church music.

No musician's education was considered complete without a visit to Italy, where Rome and Bologna were supreme in religious music and Naples in opera. Leopold took Wolferl to Italy when he was fourteen. In Rome he went to the Sistine Chapel to hear the famous *Miserere* performed during Holy Week. It was forbidden to remove the music from the chapel in any manner. Listening intently, Wolferl rushed home and wrote down every note of the complicated music. A brief second visit to scribble a few corrections completed the job. His feat became known, and one of the singers declared it to be a perfect reproduction. The Pope, far from excommunicating Wolferl, gave him a gold medal and made him a "Cavaliere." In Bologna, locked in a workroom, he passed a test for a polyphonic work in forty minutes; other musicians usually took about three hours. He was elected to the Bologna Philharmonic Academy, the youngest member in its history. All Italy recognized his genius. Once again, however, Leopold wrote, "One must be content with admiration and applause in lieu of payment."

Already Wolferl showed powers of concentration when composing. He wrote his sister from Milan, "Above us there is a violinist, below us another, next to us a singing master who gives lessons, in the last room opposite us an oboist; that makes it fun to compose, gives me many ideas." He complained, though, that his fingers ached from constant use at the keyboard or with the opera he was writing. The opera, *Mitridate, King of Ponto,* was his first to get a full-scale public production and showed his keen grasp of operatic technique. Here too he encountered jealousy. How could an Austrian (a mere child) write a successful Italian opera? How could he hope to continue the strong Italian operatic traditions of Alessandro Scarlatti and Giovanni Pergolesi (1710-1736)?

When Wolfgang was sixteen he returned to Salzburg for six unhappy, sullen, dissatisfied years. The notoriously stingy Archbishop of Salzburg gave all the best court positions to foreigners, keeping Wolfgang on as court organist at miserable pay. His only worthwhile commissions came from Milan or Munich. One of the most beautiful of his works, the *Alleluia,* was written during this unhappy period. By the time he was twenty-one, Wolfgang was a wonderfully trained, highly gifted composer, a great piano virtuoso, with no position or even the prospect of one. When the Archbishop refused him permission to go to Paris, Wolfgang resigned suddenly. His father had to stay, but insisted that his mother accompany him to Paris. Leopold knew how poorly Wolfgang could cope with life when alone. He feared he might offend important people, fall in with bad company, or spend money foolishly.

It was during this trip that Wolfgang met and fell in love

with a poor young singer, Aloysia Weber. His letters home, up to now, had always been boyish, full of clowning and clever humor; now he pleaded seriously for permission to marry Aloysia. He longed for adulthood and the chance to make his own decisions and plans for his future. But Leopold either did not recognize this hunger or chose to ignore it. The father's letters were full of anger, flattery, ridicule, and finally threats. Wolfgang yielded, giving up Aloysia, and moved bitterly on to Paris.

No longer a prodigy, he had a brooding, indifferent manner and was unable to flatter people. He was blunt and impatient, and failed utterly to make his mark in Paris. The more than fifty letters of recommendation he had through his father netted only a few playing invitations at great houses and some lessons. He could not stand the intrigues and disappointments on every side. When his mother died suddenly in Paris, it was a heavy blow. He sought Aloysia again on the way home, only to face still another disappointment—she turned him away.

In Salzburg once more he still, from force of habit, took his father's advice and returned to his court position. After one particularly bitter quarrel with the Archbishop, who called him "a scoundrel, a rascal, a vagabond—oh, I cannot write it all down"—one of the Archbishop's aides literally kicked him out of the room with the toe of his boot.

When Wolfgang left Salzburg for Vienna he left his dependence on his father behind him. Against his father's wishes he married Constanze, Aloysia's sister. She was frivolous, flirtatious, but good-hearted. Wolfgang had never had a stable home or quiet surroundings. They moved twelve times in the nine years of their marriage. Of their seven children, only two survived; every pregnancy and pitiful funeral put him deeper in debt. What money he earned was mostly by writing dances, which were the rage of Vienna; he turned them out quickly to meet immediate bills. When he could afford it, he composed incredible quantities of the music he wanted to write—comic operas, symphonies, chamber music. He was considered the finest pianist of his time, and wrote new concertos for every appearance, in addition to giving lessons. There were times

Wolfgang Amadeus Mozart

Wolfgang Amadeus Mozart

when he earned considerable sums, but Constanze was even less capable than he was of handling money. Basically happy together, they spent money on all their little pleasures—small parties, wine, billiards, dancing, riding, fancy clothes, and trinkets. With all their chronic lack of money Wolfgang was so good-natured that musicians even poorer than he could always rely on him for a loan.

Marriage gave Mozart back his humor, but it was a cynical and disillusioned one. His search for gaiety seemed almost a desperate one, as if that could make up for his professional failures. Vienna was a gay, flighty city, not ready for the daring harmonies, the subtle emotional undertones of his music. It never gave him the court appointment and recognition it had bestowed on composers far inferior to him. This was the great heartache of his life.

Prague, in Bohemia (now Czechoslovakia), was, musically, a very sophisticated city where two of Mozart's greatest operas, *The Marriage of Figaro* and *Don Giovanni* brought him great triumphs (but again not much money). "Here they talk of nothing else but—Figaro! They play, they sing, they whistle nothing but—Figaro!" As for *Don Giovanni,* most agree that it is not only Mozart's greatest opera, but perhaps the greatest ever written. It conveys every human emotion—suspense, anger, remorse, revenge, love, and yet is written with humor, theatrically, as a kind of tragic comedy. It has remained fresh and delightful to this day, and has never waned in popularity. The way it was written was typical of Mozart's unusual composing practices. From childhood on he had a photographic memory for sound—that is, he composed entire pieces in his head, complete in every detail, before putting a note on paper. The writing-out was completely mechanical, so that, as he once wrote to his sister, "I composed the fugue first and wrote it down while I was thinking out the prelude!" The ideas were in such completely polished form in his head that he rarely had to revise his manuscripts. When he was writing he loved to be surrounded by his friends, listening to their chatter, drinking punch, sharing pleasures and jokes with them.

Don Giovanni was to open the next night and not a single

note of the overture was yet on paper. After a gay party where he had danced, played piano, drunk toasts, he went to his room dead tired, and had his wife sit beside him, telling him stories to keep him awake, while he wrote the overture. He finished it early in the morning and sent it to the copyist. The opening curtain was delayed a half-hour until the parts arrived, with the ink still wet, to be played without rehearsal! At the evening's end, with tears in his eyes at the cheering and shouting, he addressed the audience: "My Prague friends, they understand me . . ."

There was another friend who understood him—Haydn. Theirs was one of the most beautiful and devoted friendships in musical history. How different they were. Mozart with his personality like quicksilver, with lightning changes of mood, a brilliant virtuoso, a born opera composer, living a life of disorder, debt and feverish pleasure-seeking. Haydn—calm, serene, businesslike, orderly, successful. When they met in 1789 Haydn was forty-nine, Mozart twenty-five. Mozart knew and admired Haydn's work so much that he dedicated six of his finest quartets to him. He poured into these quartets his most serious feelings, in beautifully proportioned form. "It was from Haydn that I learned to write quartets." The admiration was mutual. When the Prague opera house asked Haydn to write an opera, he sent a letter which expressed his unselfish attitude as well as his estimate of Mozart's worth: "It would be a risk to put myself in competition with the great Mozart. If I could only inspire every lover of music, especially among the great, with feelings as deep, and comprehension as clear as my own, in listening to the inimitable works of Mozart, then surely the nations would contend for the possession of such a jewel within their borders . . . I feel indignant that Mozart has not yet been engaged at any imperial or royal court. Pardon my wandering from the subject, but Mozart is very dear to me."

Haydn learned much from Mozart, for if the older composer made the string instruments the foundation of symphony-writing, it was Mozart who realized and developed the potential of the wind instruments. Mozart's last three symphonies were among his greatest works. When Haydn, who outlived Mozart by eighteen years, studied these symphonies he wrote "I have

64

only learned the proper use of wind instruments in my old age, and now I must die without turning my knowledge to account."

Johann Salomon, the man who persuaded Haydn to go to England, offered Mozart the same opportunity at the same time. Mozart, who needed that gamble for success far more than Haydn, refused to go. He somehow could not leave his beloved though ungrateful Vienna. Already, too, he had premonitions of the death that came to him just a few months later. The last years of his life were all downhill. His tiny salary could not make a dent in his pile of debts. The tone of his begging letters was painful. "If you, my best friend, forsake me, I and my poor sick wife and child are all lost together. Here I am with fresh entreaties instead of thanks—with new demands instead of payments! Oh, God! I can scarcely make up my mind to send you this letter, and yet I must! Forgive me!"

At the time of his death he was working despite severe pain, ironically, on his magnificent *Requiem,* (a special mass for the dead), which remained unfinished. His was a cheap, open-air funeral on such a stormy day that not even his wife followed the carriage to the cemetery. He was buried in a mass grave; no marker was ever added. If we do not know where his body is buried, we know that he achieved immortality through his music.

Mozart was one of those rare composers who brought every branch of homophonic music to a new height. To the symphony he gave a serene, mature quality and superb flexibility in the handling of a larger orchestra. In opera he brought characterization to new levels, translating every facet of human behavior from life into sound. His chamber music—trios, quartets, quintets, show the beauty of his melody, his profound emotions expressed with all the balance and clarity of the classical period's ideals; violinists, pianists, clarinetists would have poorer repertoires if not for Mozart. Besides his gift for melody and harmonic daring, his works are even more notable for his sense of structure and proportion that makes every note seem necessary and all his music inevitable.

The generations since his death have given Mozart the composer the deserved homage denied him throughout his short tragic life.

ludwig van beethoven

1770-1827

Beethoven was born a rebel and died a rebel. In between, his life was a mass of contrasts and contradictions every bit as dramatic and emotional as the music he wrote.

When Ludwig was born in 1770, Mozart was fourteen and a recognized prodigy with all the promise of a successful future. Ludwig's first rebellion was against the ambitions of his musician-father to turn him into a second Mozart. Well-meaning but overly severe, the father succeeded in making Ludwig hate his music lessons. He showed his musical ability early, learning piano and violin; he was only able to attend a very inferior school in their town of Bonn, Germany for a short time. He had an unhappy childhood in a pitifully poor home. He was short, not handsome, silent—with every excuse for becoming a failure. Even the claim that he was two years younger than he really was did not make his single "prodigy" trip resemble Mozart's in any way.

In his early teens Ludwig began serious composition study with the court organist and became his assistant, as well as a member of a theater orchestra. He obtained leave to study with Haydn in Vienna, but that did not work out well. He began to show so much originality as well as supreme self-confidence that he could not be bound by composing rules. One of his teachers, revealing his lack of judgment, warned, "Have nothing to do with him. He has learned nothing and will never do anything in decent style."

By seventeen, however, he was building his reputation as a pianist, not in the smoothly flowing style of Mozart but with a wild, forceful style that was totally new. Especially impressive was his gift for improvising on the piano, that is, taking a musical idea given to him and weaving a whole composition around it. People forgot his squat figure, the pock marks on his face, his coarse clothes and general awkwardness when they heard him perform his magic at the keyboard. At about this time he improvised a set of variations with Mozart present. "Keep your eyes on that fellow," Mozart whispered to a friend, "One day he will give the world something to talk about." Seventeen was a crowded year for Ludwig. His mother died, and his father's love of drink finally became chronic drunkenness. Ludwig had to petition the court to pay half of his father's earnings to himself; in effect, he became head of the family of three children.

The next few years were notable mainly for the free and easy terms on which the Elector of Bonn and his musicians got along. Ludwig was never afterwards awed by rank. They also marked his first friendships with the Breunings and the Waldsteins, upper-class, cultured families. They recognized Ludwig to be somewhat eccentric but appreciated his talent enough to overlook his loud voice and coarse manners.

When Ludwig went to Vienna at twenty-two, his letters from Count Waldstein gave him immediate entry to the homes of the more liberal and music-loving aristocracy. Since public concerts were still a rarity, it was at chamber and orchestra concerts in these homes that Ludwig amazed his listeners with his daring and brilliant improvisations. Count Lobkowitz put an orchestra at his disposal, Count Lichnowsky housed him for a while, and always helped with money when Ludwig needed it. He became the darling of a wide circle of these rich families, many of whom were themselves fine musical amateurs. They were especially overwhelmed by the deep feeling and grandeur of his playing of slow works; when he waxed dramatic, the strings and keys of the delicate Viennese pianos flew about. He eventually acquired a heavier piano that could supply the power and ferocity as well as the tenderness he demanded of the instrument.

The great German poet Goethe once wrote, after meeting Ludwig, "I have never seen an artist more concentrated, energetic and intense. I can understand quite well that his relationship to the world must be a strange one." He was unbelievably rude, not just to strangers whom he felt did not recognize his abilities, or to musicians who were inferior to him, but even to his best friends. Let a whisper occur while he was playing at the Lobkowitz home—"I'll play no more for such hogs," he shouted, and stalked out of the house, enraged, leaving a roomful of disappointed admirers behind. He did the same thing when someone at another party asked him innocently if he "also understood the violin." When a prince did not seat him at the royal table at a dinner he insulted the hostess and left the house on foot. He was especially rude to other musicians, treating them as he would never allow himself to be treated. At the end of one of those slow improvisations that had melted his audience to tears he laughed aloud, ridiculing the emotion he had aroused, "You're a pack of fools!"

Yet he never lost a friend, they always remained loyal and forgiving. Evidently Beethoven had a kind of personal magnetism that drew people to him despite his roughness of appearance and his suspicions and temper. They could sense the creative volcano beneath his unattractive surface; the utter integrity, sincerity and simplicity of the man shone through. They felt that his self-confidence was justified, that he was truly a genius, even before he had begun to write the masterpieces that proved it. They sensed that he really could not control his emotions, that he was a man of moods, capable in the same day of great generosity, kindness and sensitivity as well as harshness,

68

fits of temper, or cruel sarcasm. They were amused by his antics which they felt were a cover-up for self-conscious shyness.

Haydn had dedicated works in gratitude to his royal patrons; Mozart dedicated works to royalty in the vain hope that they would *become* his patrons; Beethoven dedicated many works to royal persons simply because they were friends who appreciated and helped his career (and it is because of those dedications that we remember them today). He changed the entire relationship between aristocrats and the artist; they had to accept him on his terms or not at all. When several of these royal friends cooperated to provide a regular income for him, no one thought for a moment that they were employing him, or could restrict him in any way. They were merely helping him to fulfill his rightful role in life of being able to play and write his music.

The music world itself was somewhat different since the brief few years when Mozart had passed unappreciated through it. The rising middle-class began to make public concerts possible. There were also new middle-class amateurs ready to buy music for the first time; thus music publishing began on a large scale. When Beethoven added these new sources of income to the fund set up by his friends, he was able to write to his brother, "This and the good sale of my works relieves me of all worries regarding my livelihood. Everything that I write now I can immediately sell five times over and get a good price for it as well." One of his first songs, *Adelaide,* ran to fifty editions. After only three years in Vienna he was living very well and able to send for his brothers.

He wanted to get married and seemed to be constantly in and out of love. Evidently there were many women who could not resist the force of his personality and his genius. But none of the several to whom he proposed marriage ever accepted. Most of them were of noble birth and perhaps their families objected. It is not known for certain; Beethoven did not have Mozart's great ability in letter-writing. His letters, full of bad puns, rhymes and strange spellings, tell us little of his composing processes, his thoughts on music and his personal relationships. Most tantalizing of all are a group of love letters addressed to his

"Immortal Beloved," undated and never mailed, which were found in his desk after his death. Many books have been written on the subject in an attempt to identify her.

Most of all he wanted to be a father, and tried to be one to his brothers. Here his contradictory personality made him fail miserably, causing him to repeat his father's mistakes. He tried hard to have them do what he felt was for their own good. They ended up resenting his interference in their lives, marrying out of spite women he disapproved of, and reacting to his overpowering love with bitter quarrels and family strife.

Handel was Beethoven's favorite composer. He once said, "I would go before him on my knees, uncovering my head," touching the floor with one knee as he said it. In Beethoven's early music the influences of Haydn and Mozart are strong. He used their classical forms, testing and expanding them with his own more free approach. His music seemed more personal and expressive of his inner self, than Mozart's. He did not hold back. Even his earliest compositions for the piano have more massive sounds, making greater virtuoso demands on the performer. His later piano works make that instrument sound like a whole orchestra.

The approach of the nineteenth century saw great changes in Europe in the minds of men and in the works of all artists—composers, writers or painters. "Romanticism" came to full flower. It represented a loosening of political restraints that was reflected in revolutions both in France and the United States, a new growth of trade and commerce which resulted in a fast-growing middle class, and a new awareness of the dignity and worth of the individual. Artists expressed their own emotions, and used human, immediate subjects rather than historical ones. Glorifying the rights and unique qualities of each individual led to glorifying certain outstanding ones—making "heroes" of them. The early 1800's was an age of heroes, and Beethoven's works in those years were not only heroic in style but often used heroes as their themes.

Almost all Beethoven's great works came out of this period. His *Violin Concerto,* his only opera, *Fidelio,* the oratorio *Mount*

70

Ludwig van Beethoven

of Olives, magnificent chamber music, most of his symphonies and all of his piano concertos were composed during these years. In the glorious *Fifth Symphony* he seems to portray the struggle of every man to come to terms with his fate, to rise above the trials of life to a personal triumph. In certain works, Beethoven names the hero for us, but the theme usually relates to the struggle for individual freedom. The *Egmont* overture, for example, is about the struggle of an oppressed people for liberty, told through the story of one brave leader. *Coriolanus,* based on a play by Shakespeare, depicts a ruler of such strong will that he disregarded the will of his people, thus leading to his own downfall. The opera *Fidelio* celebrates the joys of true personal devotion and the overthrow of a tyrant by brave individual sacrifice.

His third symphony, the *Heroic,* was the work that, in the words of one music critic, "threw music into the nineteenth century." When he first wrote it, Beethoven dedicated it to Napoleon in the belief that he was bringing a new political freedom to France and inspiring all Europe to similar action. When he learned that Napoleon had declared himself Emperor, he seized the title page in a fury, destroyed it and changed the name of the symphony to the *Heroic,* saying in his rage, "So he is no more than a common mortal! Now he will tread under foot all the rights of man, indulge only his own ambition; now he will become a tyrant!"

Beethoven's way of composing was completely different from that of any of the composers before him. As abrupt and careless as he was in his speech and in human relationships, as daring and imaginative as he was when improvising at the piano, he was the opposite when it came to composing. When asked where his ideas came from he said, "They come uncalled for . . . I could grasp them with hands in the open air, in the woods, while walking, in the stillness of the night or at early morning. Sometimes the moods which the poets express in words come to me in tones. They ring out, storm and rage until they finally stand before me in notes."

But between these ideas and the final composition came an

incredible amount of painstaking, careful sifting, weighing, accepting and rejecting until he felt he had found their perfect expression. A fascinating revelation of how he polished each idea over and over can be found in the many notebooks he left. Far from hearing a work whole in his mind as Mozart did, he practically rewrote every bar of music dozens of times until he was satisfied. There are eighteen versions of a certain passage in his opera *Fidelio.*

Beethoven was the first great composer who wrote with an eye to the future, aware that his works would be published and played long after he was dead. For present and future performances he added to his scores detailed instruction for performers, more than anyone before him had done. He must have anticipated that pianists of the romantic period would let themselves go, putting more of themselves than of the composers into their performances. To insure faithful interpretation, he told them exactly how fast, how slow, how soft, how loud, and with what mood every passage should be played.

It was fortunate that his instrumental works were appreciated and published and he received new commissions from musical organizations. With Napoleon's advance into Austria and eventually Vienna, the old aristocratic families began to crumble and go bankrupt; it became the public's turn to sustain Beethoven. And how proud they were of him! Mr. Stein, who owned a music store, had only to mention that he was expecting the great composer and a throng of worshipping admirers crowded his store and the street for a glimpse of him.

These years, which should have been glorious years of triumph, were marked instead by the beginning of a twenty-year struggle against deafness. No one knew of this tragic statement of his feelings, which Beethoven wrote as early as 1802, until, as he directed, it was read after his death. "I could not prevail upon myself to say to men 'Speak louder, shout, for I am deaf.' Oh, how could I possibly admit to being defective in the very sense which should have been more highly developed in me than in other men, a sense which once I possessed in its most perfect form? . . . Oh, I cannot do it."

73

"My affliction is all the more painful to me because it leads to such misinterpretations of my conduct. Recreation in human society, refined conversation are denied to me. I must live like an exile . . . What a humiliation when someone standing next to me heard a flute in the distance and I heard nothing . . . Such occurrences brought me to the verge of despair."

"I might easily have put an end to my life. Only one thing, art, held me back. Oh, it seems impossible to me to leave this world before I have produced all that I felt capable of producing, and so I prolonged this wretched existence . . . The cherished hope which I had of being healed at least to a certain degree must now abandon me entirely . . . O Providence, let a single day of untroubled joy be granted to me!"

He once conducted a concert of his own works and had to be turned around to see the thunderous applause he did not know had started (the public then realized his deafness for the first time). He began to fear that in playing with an orchestra he might get out of step with them. His attempt to conduct his opera resulted in total chaos. He knew his career as performer and conductor was over. Now he would be a composer only.

By 1815 everything bad in his life reached a climax. His brother died; he tried to adopt his nephew legally and only succeeded after a bitter court battle which lasted several years. His poor health became chronic; his sources of money began to dry up; his emotional life was one of utter frustration. In a few brief years all this soured him into a hopeless, desperate bitterness. He developed a greed for money, although he never seemed to be extravagant (later it was found that much of his conniving, even cheating of publishers, was done so that he could leave a large legacy for his beloved nephew). His suspicion of his friends became stronger than ever, he cared little about his appearance and that of his rooms.

In his last years, all his conversations were carried on in writing—almost a hundred and fifty of these "conversation books" were written in various quarters that were indescribably sordid. Music, clothes, linens were scattered over the floor, everything covered with thick dust, remains of meals, broken crockery, spilled ink pots were everywhere. He wrote one of his

74

best friends, "Don't come to see me again," calling him, "a treacherous dog." He repented bitterly the next day and wrote, "You are an honest fellow, and now I see you were right. Come then, to me, this afternoon."

Even in those last years, however, he made occasional attempts to be courteous, even charming to visitors, to accept help without furious resentment. But everything had become clearly secondary to his music, into which he poured the heroism he lacked in everyday life. The works of his last years were among his very finest. In them he rose above his pain, revealed his love of life which no amount of grief could kill. He once said he wrote out of a feeling that he had been chosen by God to express divinity through sound.

His *Ninth Symphony,* with its flexible handling of the orchestra, its titanic power and grandeur, became the ideal of all nineteenth century music. In it, he wanted to be certain that his call for brotherhood and the fulfillment of the noblest ideals would be understood by everyone. He took the revolutionary step of adding a chorus and soloists for the purpose of singing the inspiring poem *Ode to Joy.* His great *Solemn Mass* also came out of this period, as well as his last string quartets. The form of these was so original, the musical thoughts so compressed, that his contemporaries could not appreciate them. When told that one of the quartets recently performed had not been well received, Beethoven replied calmly, "They will like it some day." Only now are these works beginning to be fully appreciated and understood as among the greatest works in all music.

Beethoven felt more at home in writing for instruments than for voice. His brilliant and original piano concertos became models for several generations of composers. His piano music in general helped make that instrument the favorite one of the romantic period. His symphonies established the ideal for that form for a century after he wrote them. His wonderful flexibility in handling rhythms and shades of expression; his sudden changes in tempo; the way he intertwined melody and harmony into a single, effective whole; his imaginative harmonies; his expressive magic in writing for the orchestra; the new im-

75

portance he gave to certain instruments such as the kettledrums and doublebasses; the greatly increased length and scope of his quartets and symphonies; the range and depth of emotions he was able to convey in sound only begin to explain his greatness and importance in the development of music.

When he died at the age of fifty-seven, after sitting up in bed at the last moment to clench his fist defiantly in the direction of heaven, 20,000 mourners lined the streets for his funeral procession. In 1970, at the two-hundredth anniversary of his birth, the whole world remembered and celebrated his memory, thankful that the noblest ideals of man had found in him a great musical spokesman. Today his art continues to enrich the spirit of all who listen.

franz schubert

1797-1828

During Beethoven's last illness a friend brought him some sixty songs by a Viennese composer. He could scarcely believe that this man of thirty years had written over 500 songs— and such songs! He studied them for days, through his pain, finally exclaiming enthusiastically "He has the divine spark." The young composer, who had worshipped Beethoven from afar, haunted the inns where his idol ate, never had the courage to approach him. Despite the fact that the two had never met, Beethoven's friends, recognizing his musical stature, invited the shy young man to serve as one of the torchbearers at Beethoven's funeral. Ironically, he was himself dead by the next year. His name was Franz Schubert.

One of the few survivors of fourteen brothers and sisters, Franz had a happy childhood. His father conducted a school in their home, teaching all subjects including music. He taught Franz violin sufficiently well for him to join in string quartet playing which was the favorite family recreation. Franz soon absorbed a little viola, piano and organ too. When they played together he soon proved to be the most sensitive musically. As his brother later wrote "Whenever a mistake was made, no matter how small, he would look the guilty one in the face . . . If Papa, who played the cello, was in the wrong, he would say quite shyly and smilingly 'Sir, there must be a mistake somewhere!' and our good father would be gladly taught by him."

There may not always have been quite enough to eat, since Napoleon's soldiers stripped Vienna of food, but there was plenty of music and family devotion. The real pinch for food (and money) came later, when Franz, as choirboy in the Imperial Chapel, attended an academy attached to the University of Vienna. In the earliest of his letters, written when he was in his early teens to his elder brother, he said, "You know from experience that we all like to eat a roll or a few apples sometimes, the more so if after a middling lunch one may not look for a miserable evening meal for eight and a half hours . . . the few groats I receive from Father go to the deuce the very first few days, and what am I to do for the rest of the time?"

Constant cold, as well as hunger, made him dislike the school intensely, yet Franz remained as sweet-tempered, good-natured and amiable as when he was a child. The key to his contentment was the many opportunities he had to engage in singing, playing, conducting the school orchestra, and composing. For already, against his father's wishes, Franz knew composing was his destiny. When he was eleven a court musician had tried to teach him elements of musical composition. "If I wanted to instruct him in anything new, he already knew it. Therefore I gave him no actual instruction but merely talked to him and watched him with silent astonishment."

By thirteen he was in a positive frenzy of creative energy. The thoughts poured out faster than he could afford to buy music paper on which to write them. A university student named von Spaun, who also played in the school orchestra, was so awed by the music on hand-ruled scraps of paper which Schubert played for him that he began supplying Franz with music paper and concert tickets. This friendship lasted throughout Franz's life. Von Spaun was but the first of a number of friends and

78

admirers who eagerly helped the impractical Schubert to cope with the problems of everyday living.

His first great crisis came at sixteen, when his father insisted that he become a teacher, the only road to financial security he could see for his son. With great reluctance and with a mass of musical works already written, Franz went to a teacher-training school for a while before returning home to become his father's assistant. Teaching was sheer torture. He was a failure as a teacher and resented every moment that it took from composing. Some of his early works received performances, but his most extraordinary achievement was a song he wrote when he was seventeen (a year in which he often wrote six, seven, eight songs a day). *Gretchen at the Spinning-Wheel* is one of the greatest songs Schubert ever wrote—greater than the more famous *Erl-King* which he wrote the following year.

Taking its text from Goethe's play *Faust,* which had not yet been performed in Vienna, the song expresses the thoughts and deepest feelings of a young girl. It expresses them with artistry, with such perfect blending of voice and piano, such sympathy and tenderness in every note, that it is incredible to realize it is the work of a young, inexperienced youth. It only becomes believable on recalling that *Erl-King* was written when Schubert was eighteen. It is a dramatic, heart-breaking song of parental love and tragedy, shattering in its intensity, and is almost a miniature five-minute opera. There is an account of how he wrote it (the text, as usual, was supplied him by friends who combed the best of German poetry for their beloved Franz). "He paced up and down several times with the book, suddenly he sat down, and in no time at all there was the glorious ballad on the paper . . . on the very same evening, *Erl-King* was sung and enthusiastically received."

This manner of writing lasted all his life. His speed was so intense that it was described as "hurling" the notes on paper. He never checked what he had written, he never looked for new poems himself—his friends continued to provide him with texts, some good, others poor. Among the more than six hundred songs he wrote are some in which he transformed poor poems into great songs. He seldom used a piano while composing.

Anywhere, surrounded by conversation and noise, he would sit bent over the music paper and the book of poems, biting his pen and drumming his fingers at the same time, continuing to write easily and fluently with hardly a single correction.

On first reading a poem he seemed to catch the mood and feeling, by the second reading the notes were already established in his mind, that his pen could hardly keep pace with his musical thoughts. A friend once asked him to set a poem entitled *Serenade* as a tribute to her sister. He read it through a few times, then said smilingly "I have it already, it is done, and it is going to be quite good." It is one of his best known and most beloved songs.

He became friends, through von Spaun, with a circle of artists, writers and musicians who were soon joined by an older man, the fine singer Johann Vogl. Calling themselves "Schubertians," they took the initiative in making Franz's songs known. They arranged musical evenings devoted entirely to his works in the homes of music-loving middle-class families (not the aristocratic circles in which Beethoven moved). These evenings, which came to be called "Schubertiads," usually featured Vogl singing Franz's latest songs. Franz often accompanied him at the piano and also played with friends and the semi-amateur members of the household the chamber music he had written specially for the evening.

He had little ability or patience in dealing with publishers. His friends arranged for occasional publication, but only perhaps a tenth of his works were printed in his lifetime. They tried to prevent Franz from selling his music outright for ridiculously small sums whenever he was short of money. It was only through their protective kindness that he was able to leave Vienna for occasional short holidays in the surrounding countryside. His deep rapport with nature was fed by these trips and found its way into many of his songs.

Schubert roomed most of the time with various friends, sometimes all sharing money, food and clothing. No matter where he lived his habits remained the same—writing furiously all morning, "as soon as I finish one piece I start another"—

Franz Schubert

then out to one of his favorite cafés to meet his friends, lingering all afternoon over lunch, wine and talk, with time out for a stroll through the city streets. In the evening—music-making at a "Schubertiad."

He tried several times to acquire a royal patron, but his reputation for irregular habits and inability to follow anyone's routine but his own must have preceded him, for he never succeeded in his quest. On the two occasions when he went for brief summer stays to a small Hungarian court he could hardly wait to get back to his beloved Vienna and the circle of friends he could not live without. He wrote to a friend, "Here I have to be everything at once. Composer, editor, audience and goodness knows what besides. There is not a soul here with a genuine interest in music . . . Do not be afraid that I shall stay away longer than I absolutely must . . . My best and favorite form of entertainment is to read your letters through a dozen times."

Thus, while none of his friends were wealthy, they managed to keep him fed and clothed. Most of all they fed his spirit, treating him as a musical treasure of their own discovery, introducing him to romantic ideas and romantic poetry. He had a notion that opera-composing was the way to make money. He wrote no less than fourteen operas, some containing beautiful music. But he could not judge a good libretto (play written for an opera), and always ended up with an undramatic hodge-podge no opera director would consider. He did not know how to worm his way into the good graces of singers, directors, or other people of influence who might have arranged to have more of his operas accepted.

Perhaps it was his particularly deep disappointment at one of these operatic failures that wore down his health. He spent several months in a hospital when he was twenty-six. One of his most beautiful song-cycles (a series of songs connected by a single theme) called *The Miller's Daughter* was written in the hospital. He wrote in despair to a friend, "Picture to yourself someone whose most brilliant hopes have come to naught . . . so it seems that I have composed two more operas for nothing."

His health in his last years never restored itself completely, and his finances too took a turn for the worse, but the feverish

82

composing went on. One of his most magnificent song cycles, *Winter Journey,* was written in his last year. These songs show new depths of feeling, his early strain of melancholy becoming more gloomy, even tragic. His friends finally arranged a benefit concert for him a year before his death, the only public concert of his works ever held. He must have had a sense of the approaching end which led him to complete not only his song cycles, but also his greatest symphony, a string quintet, a Mass and three piano sonatas, all in the last few months. A week before his death (from typhoid) at thirty-one he wrote a friend, "I am ill. I have eaten nothing for eleven days and drunk nothing, and I totter feebly and shakily from my chair to bed and back again." He then asked this friend for some books by the American writer, James Fenimore Cooper, to distract him.

Even his closest friends, shocked and appalled by his death, did not fully realize the extent of their loss. Later composers spent many years persistently rummaging through drawers where Schubert had shoved completed manuscripts, ransacking the houses of friends to whom he had given many compositions, in order to bring his fantastic musical legacy to light. Once Schubert had said, more seriously than jokingly, "The state should keep me. I have come into the world for no purpose but to compose." He felt intensely that he was simply doing what came naturally, not for fame or for the future. With his quiet modesty, he had no yearning for public applause. His name was totally unknown outside of Austria. It was only gradually, as masterpiece after masterpiece was uncovered, some waiting as long as a hundred years, that the full force of his genius was realized.

Above all, the world was amazed by the quantity and quality of his purely instrumental works. The early piano pieces and dances he wrote for the "Schubertiads" are among his most delightful works. His chamber music had been performed throughout his life, but was not published and available to the music world until many years later. Of them all the *String Quintet in C,* written in his last year, is considered among the finest chamber works in musical history. Musicians for years refused to play his very long, complex and powerful *Seventh Symphony,* considering it too difficult. Its performance was postponed many times before it earned a permanent place in the concert halls of the world.

But of all his instrumental works, best known and best loved is the *Unfinished Symphony.* It is not known why it remained unfinished—whether some of it was lost, or whether Schubert ever intended to finish it. It is a gem worthy of standing next to Beethoven's great works. Schubert's rhythms have great power and drive. He loved to divide up a single melody like a conversation among different instruments, and he gave new importance to the woodwind section. Using the classical forms of Haydn, Mozart and Beethoven, the stamp of Schubert is on every melancholy melody, in his brilliant handling of harmonies, and in the sheer originality of his treatment of musical materials. If anything, he suffered from an over-abundance of melodic ideas which were hard to bring under control.

There had been fine song-writers before Schubert, particularly in England, where as far back as the 1500's William Byrd and John Dowland (1563-1626) had written boldly original, imaginative works for solo voice which marked milestones in the history of song. Haydn, Mozart and Beethoven had each written some songs, but they were all clearly much more involved with compositions of larger scope.

If Schubert had never written a note aside from his songs, he would still be one of the great heroes of music. The songs were based on poems of many German poets plus some by Shakespeare (*Hark, Hark, the Lark,* and *Who is Sylvia?*). Above all they are beloved for their melodies which cover the total range of human emotion, loneliness, sorrow, fear, joy, carefree light-heartedness, tender love, and rage. Most of the songs are lyrical, but some are dramatic, pictorial, humorous, or philosophical.

His treatment of the piano parts, sometimes simple, sometimes extremely difficult, is equally masterful. In *Gretchen* the piano is the spinning wheel; in *Erl-King,* horses's hoofs; in *The Trout,* the flashing of fish in the sparkling water. There are many realistic effects of crickets, leaves rustling, bells, birds,

84

splashing oars, calm sea, ghostly feelings, moonlight, the stillness of night, and daybreak. Some are as simple as folk songs; many are only one effective page long. Schubert even uses silence wonderfully to create feelings of suspense. The piano does not "accompany" the voice part but acts as its equal partner, both working together to extract the last drop of meaning and feeling from the poem.

Song was one of the most popular forms of composition among the romantic composers of the nineteenth century. There was not a single composer who did not owe the model and inspiration for his songs to the greatest song-composer of all time—Franz Schubert.

the romantic composers

A Handful of Heroes

There is no fixed date with which we can say, "that was when the Romantic period began." Many scholars of music think Beethoven and Schubert were as much romantic as classic composers. They point out romantic tendencies as far back as Bach and Mozart. There are composers today who still write in the romantic tradition, but the peak of Romanticism occurred in the nineteenth century; four of the five great composers in this chapter were all born between 1803 and 1811.

What is Romanticism? Coming after the balanced and rigid formal structures of classicism, it was a new way of looking at all the arts, as well as life, with curiosity and daring, with a new freedom to express the individual's ideas and feelings. It put emotion ahead of form. In music it meant inspiration might come not only from sounds themselves, but also from nature, literature, painting, philosophy, or myths. Above all, Romanticism was intensely personal. That is why the music of each romantic composer is unique. It is the product of his personality and his experiences.

FELIX MENDELSSOHN
1809-1847

Felix Mendelssohn was one of the few composers born to wealth. He was, however, far from spoiled. The well-educated parents imposed on the Mendelssohn children an incredible schedule of study that covered subjects from music to languages, all taught by private tutors or the parents themselves. By the time he was twelve, Felix was a fine artist, wrote vivid letters, spoke several languages, had the poise and self-confidence of a much older person, and was a skilled musician. He could easily have been a concert prodigy like Mozart, his parents, however, only permitted him to make a few early public appearances. Typically, when he began to compose at a young age, his parents provided a small orchestra in the theater on the family estate for him to conduct and to play his orchestral pieces.

All of this helps us to understand, at least in part, how he was able to write one of the finest works of his life when he was seventeen, the overture to *Midsummer Night's Dream.* This music, still classical in form and perfect in its use of the orchestra, was romantic in its choice of subject matter (based on Shakespeare's play), but above all for its magical atmosphere of elves and fairies. No composer since has managed to capture so completely such an airy, other-worldly quality.

In his short life (he died at thirty-eight), Mendelssohn accomplished much. He single-handedly revived interest in Bach, became a great pianist, conductor and teacher, and wrote many works in the bigger classical forms such as symphonies and chamber music. They were all imbued with his particular delicacy and grace. He wrote many solo songs, including the popular *On Wings of Song,* as well as choral music. Of the latter, the oratorio *Elijah* is best known. Openly modeled on choral styles of Handel and Bach, it anticipated some of Richard Wagner's romantic orchestral effects by many years.

It was his *Songs Without Words,* short piano pieces each expressing a single mood, that showed him at his romantic best.

They bear such titles as *Regret, Confidence, Consolation, Restlessness, Serenade* and *Flight.* In them, as in his overtures based on scenes from nature, are his finest traits—gaiety, charm, lyric melody, restrained emotion.

His clarity and good taste, and the new sounds he drew from the orchestra, brought him the same kind of musical reverence in England as Handel had earned a century earlier. Other composers such as Charles Gounod (1818-1893) in France and Peter Tchaikowsky (1840-1893) in Russia were influenced by his brand of "low-keyed" romanticism.

FREDERIC CHOPIN
1810-1849

There is hardly a single title such as Mendelssohn gave his works in the enormous piano output of Frederic Chopin. This Polish-French composer was born just one year after Mendelssohn. He disdained giving the slightest clue to his feelings by words. He wanted the notes themselves to convey his emotional messages. The darling of the Polish nobility, he played before the court from the age of eight. His first compositions were published when he was fifteen. Chopin soon realized that his beloved Poland was a dead end musically. The great musical capitals of Vienna and Paris beckoned, and it was in Paris that he lived the last half of his life, from twenty-one to thirty-nine. The great German poet Heinrich Heine wrote of him, "Chopin was born in Poland of French parentage and was partly educated in Germany . . . Poland gave him his historical sorrow, France his grace, Germany his romantic melancholy; and nature gave him a slim, charming, somewhat delicate appearance."

His aristocratic bearing matched a certain almost snobbish aloofness and reserve in his personality. Extremely sensitive to people and surroundings, he was not a pianist for the masses.

Frederic Chopin

Felix Mendelssohn

Often called the "poet of the piano," he found his most congenial environment in the salons of the Parisian nobility. A close friend once described his life, "He visited several salons every day, or he chose at least every evening a different one. He had thus by turns twenty or thirty salons to intoxicate or to charm with his presence."

What enthralled his hearers and inspired them to take lessons from him at very high fees, were both his music and his way of playing it. Behind the mask of such neutral names as *Waltz,* or *Prelude,* or *Nocturne,* lay exquisite emotions, melancholy or gay, playful or violent, portrayed by a completely original and imaginative use of the piano, (Chopin wrote almost exclusively for that instrument). Rippling, lacy patterns, sometimes as fine as spider-webs, were spun over the entire keyboard, which had only recently been enlarged to its present size. His brilliant and daring harmonies were enhanced by his revolutionary use of the pedals for entirely new effects. There is hardly a trace of the classical forms; he invented his own as he needed them. His rhythm innovations alone entitle him to the status of a hero. He made *rubato* an important part of the romantic music scene. This was a momentary disregard of the strict tempo, a freer spacing of the beats, that made rhythm more elastic and expressive. His long, spun-out melodic lines were full of ornaments that were part of the musical thought, not tacked on "for show" as were the ornaments added by so many pianists and singers of the time.

His ideas came to him as easily as did Mozart's, but putting them into final form was as difficult for him as it had been for Beethoven. "He shut himself up in his room for whole days, weeping, walking, breaking his pens, repeating and altering a bar a hundred times . . . with desperate perseverance. He spent six weeks over a single page." And desperate indeed was the race between his creative energy and the slow death from tuberculosis which embittered the last few years of his life.

Chopin was the first well-known composer to come from the eastern, Slavic part of Europe. Practically self-taught both as pianist and composer, he was a genius whose talents, like

90

Mozart's, defy explanation. No other composer was ever able to imitate him with any success, but many of his piano devices, harmonies and pedal effects crept into other composers' works from then on. Not all of Chopin's works are delicate ripples of sound in subtle rhythmic patterns, or poignant melodies. Some are passionate outpourings of tumultuous sound. His *Mazurkas, Polonaises* and *Waltzes* reflect the influence of his early Polish years. Some of them deal powerfully with Polish folk material, giving us a glimpse of a very different music he might have written if he had remained longer in his native land.

ROBERT SCHUMANN
1810-1856

In the first issue of the *New Journal of Music* which the composer Robert Schumann founded in 1834, he wrote, in a glowing article on Chopin, "Hats off, Gentlemen. A genius!" Generous praise indeed of one composer for another, especially since they were both exactly the same age, twenty-four. Schumann was among the most romantic of all composers in his outlook. He idealized friendship and love, yet he could not stand being contradicted, and could be violent towards such composers as Gioacchino Rossini (1792-1868) and Giacomo Meyerbeer (1791-1864) for what he felt to be the insincerity and shallowness of their music.

He turned to music late, since his parents had insisted on his studying law. He wrote to his mother when he was twenty, "Now I stand at the crossroads and am frightened by the question: where to? If I obey my genius, it directs me towards art . . . but actually, I have always felt as though you were barring my way . . . Write to Wieck (his piano teacher) yourself, and ask him plainly what he thinks of me and my plans for the future . . . this is the most important letter I have ever written or shall ever write."

Frederick Wieck, a fine musician and thorough teacher, tipped the scale in favor of music. Schumann, however, never achieved his earliest musical ambition, to become a concert pianist. In trying to make up for his late start in piano study he invented a gadget to help stretch his fingers. It succeeded only in permanently crippling his hand, so that he had to turn entirely to composing music instead.

At age twenty-six, he and Wieck's seventeen-year-old daughter were hopelessly in love. Her father strongly opposed the match and they could not marry until she became twenty-one, after years of legal battles. Clara Wieck was a child prodigy who later became one of the greatest women pianists. Just as idealistic as Robert, she shunned the exhibition pieces dearly prized by the showman-pianists, playing instead Bach, Beethoven and, most of all, Schumann. In the forty years she outlived her husband, Clara fought and finally succeeded in making his music known and loved as it never was in his lifetime.

Their marriage, glowing and happy, was one of tender love and devotion. Clara gave up her career temporarily to raise a family and help Schumann in his work. He had composed a great deal before, but the marriage raised the quality and quantity of his compositions to new heights. The over two hundred songs which he wrote during the first year of their marriage marked him as the first song-writer to be compared with Schubert. The next year he concentrated on piano music. One of the great melody writers, he was at his best in short pieces in which all shades of emotion were portrayed, the title often indicating the mood. He played literary games, using the letters of Bach's name as the notes for a composition, for example, B-A-C-H; in German the note Bb is called H.

Among his most beloved piano works are those for and about children, whom he understood and loved, *Album for the Young* and *Scenes from Childhood*. The piano was his natural medium, but Clara urged him to write for the orchestra. In his symphonies we sense an uncertainty in the handling of the instruments, some parts sounding as if they would be better played on the piano. The larger forms and the leisurely development of themes seemed to make him impatient. Yet his *Piano Quintet* and *Piano Concerto* are among the gems of musical literature. Bach was Schumann's idol, and he tried to fuse thick polyphonic texture with his highly-charged, romantic musical ideas. He was one of the most intelligent, well-read and literary of all composers. In his *New Journal of Music* he fought hard for recognition of good music by new composers such as Chopin, Schubert, Mendelssohn and Hector Berlioz—more recognition than he himself achieved.

Sadly, after a few brief years of marriage his mind began to suffer. First he became morbid, hearing voices and had lapses of memory. After a suicide attempt, he spent his last years in an asylum until his death at forty-five. From there he once wrote to Clara, "How I wish I could listen to your beautiful playing again. Was it all a dream—our tour in Holland, your brilliant reception everywhere, and the torches carried in our honor?"

JOHANNES BRAHMS
1833-1897

While Schumann was still at the height of his career he had written in his diary "Brahms to see me, a genius." In this instance he showed the same keen musical judgment as he had twenty years earlier with Chopin. For Johannes Brahms, aged twenty-three, that meeting was one of the most important events in his life. Schumann's ardent support made him famous and brought publishers to his doorstep requesting new works. Brahms more than repaid Schumann by his lifelong devotion to Clara and the Schumann children, acting like a second father to them. He was also deeply in love with Clara, who was fourteen years older than he. Her devotion to Schumann's memory (among other reasons) prevented their ever marrying. These circumstances may well account for a strain of melancholy, even pessimism, in much of Brahms's life and music.

He had started life as a slum child. At the age of thirteen he helped support the family by playing piano in the cheap cabarets and saloons of Hamburg, Germany. Largely self-taught, his fine mind led him to explore continually throughout his life, every period of music. Notoriously rude, cold and sarcastic, he was quick to help and advise those whom he respected or loved. Completely unkempt in appearance, he was neat, thorough and well-organized in his composing. Even when he became very wealthy and honored he continued to live very simply.

The contradictions of his nature also extend to his music. In his earlier works he excelled in the same small gems of song and piano compositions as Schumann did. But with growing success and the urging of his public and publishers, he finally turned to his secret ambition, the writing of symphonies. What he once wrote helps us understand why his first symphony took twenty years to complete, "You have no idea how it feels to hear behind you the tramp of a giant like Beethoven." Just as Schumann became the greatest song composer since Schubert, Brahms, in his four symphonies, showed himself a worthy successor of Beethoven. Yet he is equally recognized for his *Requiem,* his chamber music, and certain miniature masterpieces such as his *Lullaby* and *Hungarian Dances.*

His earlier works were brilliant and thoroughly romantic, full of inventive ideas, imagination and wit. In later years he used more self-restraint than the other romantics, became expert in the use of the older classical forms, and produced music of a more mellow, resigned and personal effect. In all of Brahms's music there is the basic sincerity, nobility, restraint and dignity which marked his life.

HECTOR BERLIOZ
1803-1869

There was little that was noble, restrained or dignified about the Frenchman Hector Berlioz, whose romanticism was at opposite poles from that of Brahms, Chopin or Schumann. Thin and angular, with an enormous crop of red hair, his appearance was in some ways as fanciful as his personality and music. He had a fiery and morbid imagination, a great craving for love, and a history of fear and pain in human relationships. He also seemed to have a deep need to make his feelings public, almost wallowing in his miseries. He once described his reactions on hearing "good music," "My arteries quiver violently . . . tears . . . my muscles contract . . . my limbs tremble, and my feet and hands are numb. I cannot see perfectly. I am giddy and half faint."

He showed great wit, sensitivity and musical judgment in his *Autobiography* and also in his music criticism, through which he earned his living for over thirty years. But his peculiar nature drew him to themes that had never before been expressed so thoroughly in music—terror, doom, bizarre and extravagant fantasies, supernatural happenings. They are expressed most vividly in his *Fantastic Symphony.* This is not only a symphony in form, but also the first important example of "program music," (music that tells a story). In its own way it traces his life and thoughts, starting with a young, imaginative, sensitive artist, his search for the ideal woman, his dreams shattered, imagined scenes of despair, murder, delirium, witches, demons.

In speaking of this and other works Berlioz once wrote, "These compositions call for a combination of precision and verve, controlled passion, dreamy tenderness, and an almost morbid melancholy. For this reason it is extremely painful for me to hear my compositions conducted by anybody but myself." It was true that only his superb conducting seemed to do justice to his music. This was true partly because he was one of the greatest masters of all time in using each instrument of the orchestra as almost a solo instrument. He understood their strengths and weaknesses, their expressive possibilities, and exploited them fully. His book on orchestration is still valuable reading for music students today.

He could achieve delicate effects with woodwinds, as in the *Dance of the Sylphs,* almost as well as Mendelssohn. One critic

95

Robert Schumann

Johannes Brahms

Franz Liszt

said it sounded like "vanishing soap bubbles." But above all he, of all the romantic composers, "thought big." He called for orchestras twice the usual size, and wrote a *Requiem* for four separate brass ensembles in addition to the orchestra and a chorus of hundreds. He dreamed of an ideal orchestra of over four hundred instruments.

Berlioz had a small, devoted following in his day, but was too advanced in his musical ideas to be appreciated fully by the public, although eventually France conferred high honors on him. The composer Giuseppe Verdi summed up Berlioz's work, "He was greatly and subtly gifted . . . but he had no moderation. He lacked the calm and . . . the balance that produce complete works of art. He always went to extremes, even when he was doing admirable things." Among his most admirable were certainly the noble, lyrical music of his opera *The Trojans* and the haunting, lovely, mysterious oratorio, *The Childhood of Christ.*

Yet Berlioz had a great influence on the course of music history. He showed that music could be inspired directly by poetic and literary ideas, and could summon up pictures as well as moods; that individual instruments could be used vividly in new and daring ways; that it was possible to achieve massive and heroic effects by multiplying the sheer number of instruments and voices used. He was the first to use, in the *Fantastic Symphony,* a "fixed idea," (a short melodic theme associated with a particular person), in this case it was "Her," the ideal woman. Every time she appears in person in the artist's thoughts we know it by the presence of her theme. Berlioz's melodies and rhythms, highly individual, expressed the ugly and horrifying in life as well as the beautiful and good.

FRANZ LISZT
1811-1886

There was no instrument that Berlioz himself could play passably. Yet the man who benefited most from his example was one of greatest pianists of the century before he turned to composing—Franz Liszt. By thirteen Franz was the sensation of Europe from Vienna to Paris to London, and had already reached the first of several religious crises during his life when he felt that he should join the priesthood.

By twenty-two he was admired hysterically. Hundreds of women mobbed the stage frantically after every performance, ready to tear his gloves to bits for souvenirs. His wizardry at the keyboard led him to play his own dazzling arrangements of works by other composers. He tried and succeeded in recreating Berlioz's stunning orchestral effects on the piano alone. His piano works also show keen awareness of the special effects Chopin invented; but his showmanship was all his own. Tall, striking, his face by turns dreamy, tragic, amiable, captivating, he remained a popular idol even after his retirement from the concert stage.

Self-educated, Liszt mingled with the intellectual leaders of all Europe, and was on terms of equality, even superiority, with European nobility. His long professional life took many turns. He was a pianist, composer, conductor, teacher, eventually even taking minor orders in the church. Of all musicians he was the most generous in getting new music performed and in personally helping struggling composers. He taught hundreds of pianists (many without fee) and was in every sense the dominant figure of mid-nineteenth century European musical life.

His heroism in the history of music stems partly from the way he expanded the tonal possibilities of the piano. But it also rests on his orchestral compositions. He had the daring to abandon the symphonic form and create a new, free, one-movement form which united dramatic, pictorial and lyrical ideas. This was the birth of the "tone poem." He carried

Berlioz's "fixed idea" further by starting with a tiny melodic figure and making it the basis of an entire work by continually elaborating and transforming it. That single germ of an idea served to express varied actions and emotions. There had been examples of program music before. Antonio Vivaldi (in addition to Haydn) had written an instrumental work called *The Seasons* in the early 1700's. Beethoven's *Pastoral Symphony* portrayed the composer's reactions to country scenes. But Liszt and Berlioz carried program music much further along the road to realism.

Where Liszt did not quite succeed was in trying to express philosophical and religious ideas such as the conflict between good and evil. Those works, (the symphonic poem *The Ideal*, for example) have a hollowness, an insincerity that detracts from their musical value. Liszt did much to make the world aware of the riches of Hungarian folk song in his *Hungarian Rhapsodies*. Later in life he abandoned the glittering color splashes of his earlier music. He experimented with new harmonies that anticipated twentieth-century practices and had an immediate influence on many younger composers. It is by his *Hungarian Rhapsodies* and certain tone-poems such as *The Preludes* that Liszt is best remembered today.

These, then, were the outstanding romantic composers. Traces of Brahmsian romanticism were reflected in several later composers such as Sergei Rachmaninoff (1873-1943) in Russia and the English composers Sir Edward Elgar (1857-1934) and Ralph Vaughan Williams (1872-1958). In the United States Edward MacDowell (1861-1908), while using American Indian themes, still was in the Brahms tradition. In our own times Howard Hanson (1896-   ) has written a *Romantic Symphony* which is aptly named. But the Liszt-Berlioz influence was much stronger, particularly when to it was added the musical revolution created by Richard Wagner.

heroes of their countries

Romanticism took a new turn around 1815 after Napoleon's defeat. There was much discontent which erupted in uprisings, as boundary changes were made which often ignored their culture and language. Whole nations, rather than only individuals, wanted to assert their independence, to express their own feelings and national pride. Among the politically weak countries there was a desire to show their worth by using their own folk materials in art, literature and music. The music of Haydn and Mozart was written in a general European language. By the middle of the nineteenth century music began to bear a stamp that could be clearly heard, "made in Norway," or "made in Hungary."

Russia's musical history is particularly important. For centuries the nobility heard only imported Italian, French or German music played and sung mostly by foreign musicians. They knew a little about the rich heritage of music of the Greek Orthodox Church, but they had no knowledge of the varied folk music familiar to the peasants of the vast Russian empire. By the

100

end of the nineteenth century Russia had already made rich contributions to literature through their nationalist writers such as Pushkin, and had produced a spectacular body of nationalistic music.

Just as Pushkin wrote of Russian history, life and legends, so his friend Michael Glinka (1803-1857), founded Russian music on the same base. He used vigorous, fresh folk tunes in his operas *A Life for the Czar* and *Russlan and Ludmilla,* creating in them a distinctive, colorful national music. The Russian people, nobility and average man alike, were enthralled by these operas on native subjects which dealt with peasants rather than far-off historical or mythical figures.

There was no tradition of professional composers or music teachers in Russia. Public concerts were rarely held and there was no conservatory for music education until the middle of the nineteenth century. No wonder Peter Tchaikovsky, who graduated from the first conservatory in St. Petersburg, and had thorough training in the German tradition, held the other Russian composers in contempt. He called them "very gifted persons . . . infected with the worst sort of conceit and with a purely dilettantist (amateur) confidence in their superiority over all the rest of the musical world." He was largely correct. The group, often called the "Russian Five," *were* amateurs. Mily Balakirev (1837-1910), their guiding light, took pride in ignoring everything European in musical knowledge. And he was the only professional musician in the group. César Cui (1835-1918) was an engineer, Alexander Borodin (1834-1887) was a well-known physician and research chemist, Modest Moussorgsky (1839-1881) was a civil servant, and Nicolai Rimsky-Korsakov (1844-1908) was once a naval officer.

As composers they were all self-taught. Rimsky-Korsakov was thrust most unexpectedly into the position of Professor of Harmony at the new conservatory. He managed to keep just a lesson or two ahead of his pupils at first, but during the years after he gave up his naval career, he made up for lost time by teaching himself to play every instrument in the orchestra. He achieved such knowledge of their possibilities that he became a master of orchestration. His book on writing for orchestra is found alongside of Berlioz's on music students' bookshelves. Perhaps his naval experience helped him in writing music portraying the sea, in such works as *Scheherezade* and in *Sadko,* (the first tone poem written by a Russian) which dealt with a submarine kingdom. He made a collection of popular tunes, using some of them in his operas. Some were exotic, Oriental-sounding melodies from the Near East countries on Russia's borders. His *Russian Easter Overture* captured the deep, impressive sounds of the Greek Orthodox church choirs.

César Cui never wrote any particularly important music. Borodin, however, that scientific genius who also founded a school of medicine for women, wrote in his spare time at least one symphony, his second, that was a uniquely Russian masterpiece. He called himself a "Sunday musician," and never managed to finish his greatest work, the opera *Prince Igor,* which he worked on for seventeen years. Rimsky-Korsakov completed it after Borodin's death from sketches he had left. This was music of splendid barbarity which drew on the semi-Oriental musical treasures of the Asiatic provinces of Russia. The *Dances* from this opera are still great concert favorites.

But the true hero of Russian musical nationalism was Modest Moussorgsky. He started life as the son of a prince and ended it in pitiful circumstances as a hopeless drunkard at the age of forty-two. He too began his musical life as an amateur while he was an army officer. Perhaps it was the loss of the family fortune, which changed him from a wealthy landlord and owner of many peasant-serfs to a life of severe poverty that destroyed him.

As a member of the "Five" Moussorgsky learned to compose by himself or by picking up ideas and suggestions from the others. But from the beginning he showed the most daring originality, both in choice of subject matter and in treatment of musical ideas. Sometimes, like Berlioz, he wrote about supernatural happenings, as in *Night on Bald Mountain,* a tone poem portraying a night of horror among witches and other evil creatures. He could also paint pictures with sounds, as in *Pictures at an Exhibition,* in which each musical section portrays a painting by an artist friend of his. But the full force of his genius comes through in the one opera he lived to complete, *Boris Godounov*. This is not "pretty" music, but music that reaches such depths of intensity, probing the innermost thoughts, the very soul of its tragic hero. It is a triumph of musical realism and psychology, and ranks among the great musical and dramatic masterpieces.

Moussorgsky broke almost every rule of romantic opera in *Boris Godounov*, shocking his listeners at first. The principal character was actually the Russian people themselves. There was no love interest and there were few solos. The whole opera consisted of choruses and dialogue. The usual main roles for a woman singer or a tenor were missing (Boris is a bass). Even the dialogue was different, in that Moussorgsky tried to capture the rhythms of the Russian language rather than the familiar European models. The music was often harsh, the melodies odd, the rhythms strange and at times violent. Everything was secondary to the real feeling for the Russian people, their history and spirit—Moussorgsky's goal in writing the opera. His sordid life and early death after the completion of very few musical works is one of the great tragedies in the history of music.

Of all the Russian composers mentioned, the one whose works are most played today was the least nationalistic of them all—Peter Tchaikovsky (1840-1893). While he knew and loved Russian folk songs, most of his work did not stem directly from them. At his best he was a true romantic, sometimes to an extreme. A man of many moods, his *Sixth Symphony*, often called the *Pathétique*, is darkly melancholy but with moments full of power and beauty, yet the final movement of his popular *Violin Concerto* is exuberantly gay. One of his finer works was the opera *Eugen Onegin*. His *Fourth, Fifth* and *Sixth Symphonies*, as well as the *Romeo and Juliet Overture*, the first *Piano Concerto in Bb Minor*, and the *Violin Concerto* are all very much alive in the concert hall today. If Tchaikovsky had written nothing but his fairy-tale ballets *The Nutcracker, Sleeping Beauty* and *Swan Lake*, his name would still be a household word among music lovers.

Bohemia (Czechoslovakia), unlike Russia, had a long tradition of concert music. Prague, its capital, was one of the great music centers of Europe. It was Bedrich Smetana (1824-1884), its first famous composer, who captured in music the longings of the Bohemian people for freedom from Austrian and German rule. He grew up in the utmost poverty, not even able to afford an instrument. He once sent a composition, along with a pleading letter telling of his circumstances to Franz Liszt, asking for a loan to make it possible for him to continue in music. Liszt, both generous and appreciative of his abilities, replied "I should like to express my warm thanks for the dedication . . . the pieces are most outstanding and finely felt." Liszt found a publisher for him and became an ardent champion of Smetana's music.

Perhaps his greatest work was *The Bartered Bride,* a comic folk opera that reflected Bohemia's desire for independence. Sparkling and brilliant, it is one of the finest of all comic operas. Smetana, in this and other operas, invented melodies very much in the spirit of the Bohemian folk songs and dances, particularly the polka. He also wrote a series of tone poems under the general title *My Country,* which convey the feeling and scene of the Bohemian countryside. The one named for a river, *The Moldau,* is the best known. The directness of his music, its peasant vitality and vigor, put Bohemia on the musical map and instilled national pride in its people.

Just as ardent a Czech musical patriot as Smetana, and much more famous throughout the world, was the composer Antonin Dvorak (1841-1904). Antonin was a country boy who retained the simplicity of someone close to nature all his life. His father, a butcher and innkeeper, fully expected Antonin to follow in his footsteps, but the son was drawn to music from his earliest days. He learned the violin, viola, piano and organ as soon as he was exposed to them. In all his life he probably attended regular music classes for only two years. He wrote music continuously, learning by doing, destroying his early works. "I always have paper to start my fires." He made his living by playing in orchestras wherever he could, in restaurants, at

Hector Berlioz

Georges Bizet

dances, in the opera house, developing a fervent artistic and personal devotion to Czech musical traditions.

The composer Johannes Brahms was on the jury that awarded to Dvorak three years in a row the Austrian state prize for composing, and later helped him get a publisher. Brahms gave Dvorak invaluable advice, and called his compositions "my best friends." When Dvorak's *Slavonic Dances* were first heard, with their impulsive shifts from slow to fast, their great energy and singable melodies, they brought him world fame. Suddenly every musical organization sought his new works. Despite his vast fame, heightened by tours throughout Europe, and the tremendous pride he brought to Czech hearts, he continued to live modestly, and to compose enchanting symphonies, tone poems, songs and chamber music.

Eventually, he accepted an invitation to the United States, where he headed the National Conservatory of Music in New York for three years. There, among his pupils, was the black composer Harry Burleigh (1866-1949), who acquainted Dvorak with the Negro spirituals. The *New World Symphony*, which grew out of this American visit, uses one of those spirituals in its slow movement, although the symphony as a whole is much more Bohemian than American. Dvorak said in an interview that "future American music will and must be based on the plantation songs, which are typically American."

Liszt and Brahms had written works which they called "Hungarian," but to the greatest Hungarian composer, Bela Bartok (1881-1945) these were only "gypsy" music, the reflection of that gifted wandering people believed to have come originally from India. He spent summers and vacations for thirty years (along with being professor of piano at the Royal Academy of Music in Budapest) wandering through rural Hungary, collecting folk songs from peasants the way a scientist might collect rocks or butterflies. "It is not enough to study it as it is stored up in museums," he said of folk music. Later he also went as far afield as Rumania and Turkey in his search for the authentic.

He was a very quiet, withdrawn man. Although he played the piano in public at the age of ten, he hated performing.

106

Composing started early, but he earned his first fame as a folk-music scholar rather than as a composer. When he used this tremendous source of ready-made melodies he did not smoothe out or prettify them. No "skin-deep" nationalism for him. He left them as crude and rough and rhythmically irregular as he found them, but treated them to spicy harmonies that make his work very individual, strong and powerful. Born towards the end of the nineteenth century, he came at various times under the influence of Strauss, Liszt, Debussy and the American composer Henry Cowell (1897-1965). No matter how complex his music became, it always retained the biting rhythms, the sharp, sometimes ugly sounds of the true Hungarian musical spirit he strove so hard to capture. Bartok may yet become the future's choice as one of the greatest composers of our century. Appreciation of his works has grown tremendously since his death in New York in 1945. He had left Hungary three years before at great personal sacrifice, leaving his sons behind, as a protest against the politics of Hitler and Mussolini. His most popular works include a collection of short piano pieces called *Microcosmos*, a *Concerto for Orchestra, Music for Strings, Percussion and Celesta,* and six string quartets.

Bartok's best friend, Zoltan Kodaly (1882-1967) worked with Bartok on his folk song research and was himself an outstanding composer of Hungarian-inspired music. His noble and tragic *Hungarian Psalm* expressed his people's feelings under foreign occupation, and the music from his comic folk opera *Hary Janos* still delights audiences. Rumania, too, found its greatest musical spokesman in the twentieth century, in the person of Georges Enesco (1881-1955). His two very popular *Roumanian Rhapsodies* capture perfectly the distinctive mixture of gypsy, southern European and Balkan influences in the folk music of that country.

The Scandinavian countries, too, began to find their own musical voices, eventually breaking away from the German and Italian influences. In Norway, Edvard Grieg (1843-1907), sometimes called the "Chopin of the North," came from a middle-class family of good social position. He idolized the Norwegian farmer and fisherman, and studied lovingly their

107

dances and music. Some of his music, such as the very popular *Piano Concerto,* is on a grand scale, but he was at his best in his songs and his arrangements of Norwegian folk tunes. His *Lyric Pieces* for piano give us a lively view of Norwegian scenery and country life. In his suites on Norwegian myths, such as *Peer Gynt* and *In Holberg's Time,* he perhaps best captured the Norwegian folk idiom, its particular dance rhythms, its unusual scales which give it special flavor. He was a close friend of Liszt, and his delicate, lyrical style influenced composers as far away as France and England. His many international tours as a pianist, along with his wife, a singer, spread his idiom throughout Europe. Norway honored him by granting him a pension to help him continue composing. His sixtieth birthday, in 1903, was declared a national holiday.

In the years when Jan Sibelius (1865-1957) was growing up, Finland was trying desperately to free itself from Russia. He was a strange man, intensely patriotic, but more drawn to the Finnish landscape, its forests, meadows, legends, than to the people. By the time he was twenty he set about writing music based on Finnish history and myths that would remind his people of their ancient heroes and their own hidden strength. He celebrated in his music the physical beauty of Finland which meant so much to him. So well did he succeed that he has been called the "uncrowned king of Finland." His tone poem *Finlandia,* for example, so inflamed the Finnish yearning for freedom that its performance was forbidden by the Russian rulers of the country for many years. Even his symphonies, experimental though some of them were, seemed to breathe the somber melancholy of the Finnish landscape as well as the dramatic struggle of its people. The Finnish government considered Sibelius a precious national asset. Besides helping spread his fame throughout the world, the country gave him a magnificent forest home and a generous pension to enable him to continue working and living in the seclusion he cherished. He stopped writing music long before his death in 1957, but the Finnish spirit lives on in some of his works like *En Saga* and *The Swan of Tuonela* as well as some of his symphonies.

108

The story of the national music of Spain is among the most fascinating. Unlike the comparative isolation of Norway or Finland, Spain was, from the middle ages on, a melting pot of Mediterranean peoples. Waves of Moors, Jews, gypsies all left their indelible marks on her culture, and particularly on her music and dance. This combination of African and Near Eastern influences made Spanish folk music so exotic, so rhythmically exciting and melodically ornamented, that few composers anywhere in Europe could resist writing "Spanish" music once having heard it. Spain was among the less developed countries in composed music (outside of church music, which was magnificently enriched by the works of Tomás Victoria (1548-1611). It was rather peculiar that Glinka, the Russian composer, wrote *Memories of a Summer Night in Spain;* Rimsky-Korsakov composed the brilliant *Spanish Caprice;* Georges Bizet (1838-1875), a French composer, wrote his masterpiece (in French) about totally Spanish characters in a vivid style that captured the idiom of Spanish folk music—the opera *Carmen;* Maurice Ravel (1875-1937), also a Frenchman, wrote a *Spanish Rhapsody.* All of this took place while those Spanish composers who had the musical training to use their priceless heritage were heard only in Spain, remaining outside the main stream of European music.

It was not until the works of such native Spanish composers as Isaac Albeniz (1860-1909) and Enrique Granados (1867-1916) that the world realized it had been hearing tourist Spanish music which tried to capture local color, rather than the real thing. Albeniz, a piano prodigy who played his way alone around the world at the age of thirteen, depicted the varying sounds of the different Spanish provinces, each with its distinctive musical traditions in his piano suite *Iberia.* Granados used the paintings of the great Spanish artist Goya for the setting and characters of his opera *Goyescas.* An orchestral suite of selections from this opera has lasted longer than the opera itself.

Perhaps most outstanding of all the Spanish composers was Manuel de Falla (1876-1946). He was deeply influenced by new trends in French music, yet his rhythms, melodies, atmosphere

Bela Bartok

Carlos Chavez

are all intensely Spanish. Without using actual folk songs, he evokes the depths of melancholy and fire, of despair and wild abandon, that we now know are truly Spanish. His tone poem *Nights in the Gardens of Spain,* his opera *La Vida Breve (The Short Life)*, and the ballet *The Three-Cornered Hat* have carried the insistent, hypnotic beat of Spain to concert halls all over the world.

There were other countries that had a flowering of national music, such as Heitor Villa-Lobos (1887-1959) in Brazil and Carlos Chavez (1899-   ) in Mexico. In England Ralph Vaughan Williams (1872-1958) steeped himself in the study of English folk song from as far back as Shakespeare's time, using them in such works as the *Norfolk Rhapsodies* and the *London Symphony.* He perhaps best summed up the aims of a composer intensely aware of his own heritage in his book *National Music,* in which he said, "Every composer cannot expect to have a world-wide message, but he may reasonably expect to have a special message for his own people."

richard wagner
1813-1883

There was nothing heroic about Wagner as a man. He was vain, selfish, domineering, insincere, unscrupulous, and disloyal to those who befriended him. He sought publicity and would stop at nothing to claw his way to the top. He lived in luxury as long as the money he had borrowed held out. He fled Germany several times to escape imprisonment for unpaid debts. And more than once he ran off with another man's wife. Without compassion, insensitive, his obsession with German superiority made him a racist.

He was convinced he was a genius, to whom the world owed a handsome living as well as the homage usually accorded kings. Strangely enough, in a way he was right. Not only was he the most famous and talked-about musical figure of the second half of the nineteenth century, but the entire history of music from his day to recent times was dominated by him. Composers were either pro-Wagner or anti-Wagner.

His medium for composing was primarily opera, although he was dissatisfied with opera as it existed when he started composing. As far back as the middle 1700's the composer

112

Christophe Gluck (1714-1787) had tried, with only temporary success, to reform the abuses of the "star" system that placed singers above composers. The audience, arriving fashionably late in time for the second act, was noisy. They ate and talked busily in the well-lit opera houses, all but ignoring the stage during the stretches of sung dialogue, paying attention only when the show-stopping "act" of a star singer's aria was about to begin, or when the ballet scene came on. It was more a social experience than a musical one.

Wagner had not as yet developed his revolutionary ideas in his early operas. *Rienzi,* his first big success, owed much to the spectacular operas of Giacomo Meyerbeer (1791-1864), a French composer whose works dominated all of European opera in the mid-century. *The Flying Dutchman* bore an even greater influence—that of Carl Maria von Weber (1786-1826), whose opera *The Marksman* (*Der Freischutz*) caused a furor at its premiere in 1821. It was the first completely German romantic opera, written in German and based on German traditions and culture. Weber anticipated Wagner's attempts to paint the German forest in sound, among other new ideas. Weber brought a breath of fresh air to opera. Although Mozart was his model, he belonged to the new, nineteenth century nationalistic and, romantic group. In his attempt to unify music and drama, in his restless, original melodies, in his ingenious exploration of new orchestral coloring in such operas as *Euryanthe* and *Oberon,* he anticipated Wagner still further. In *The Flying Dutchman* and in *Tannhauser,* Wagner, like Weber, was moving away from the deadly aria-recitative division. The melodies follow the text in a kind of "speech-song," with the orchestra taking on a more important role.

Wagner thought at first that he would be a writer, and wrote many dramas and essays as a young man. In them he expressed some of the thoughts that caused an upheaval when he later applied them to music. He was a fanatical romanticist who felt that he had three missions in life. One was to give the German people a new mythology, to awaken heroism and superiority in them by recreating ancient pre-Christian German

113

and Nordic myths and connecting them to modern man. His was an exaggerated, dangerous form of nationalism which many years later gave support to the racist theories of Adolf Hitler, a great admirer of Wagner.

Another of his self-imposed missions was to glorify the artist, in any art. By raising the artist to the position of hero he could do anything, in life as well as in art. Perhaps that is why Wagner lived as if the laws and conduct imposed on ordinary individuals had little to do with him. Art, to this totally non-religious man, was itself a religion, and the artist its priest.

But his most important mission was to try to realize the dream of Romanticism—the uniting of all the arts into a single one. We cannot help but admire the versatility and energy he threw into this new idea, which he called "music drama" rather than "opera." That is what he called the series of four operas known as *The Ring of the Nibelungen* which, telling a complicated story of ancient gods and men, was full of symbols and psychology, natural and supernatural events, dwarfs turning into serpents, flying horses, and magic fires.

Wagner personally took charge of every aspect of opera production. He was the first composer who wrote the entire text himself. He also designed the scenery and costumes. He worked out the stage directions and designed special machinery needed for the action. He both selected and trained the new type of singers his music required. Even raising the money by tours throughout the country fell to him. He wanted an entirely different type of theater in which people could hear this "music of the future." He designed and supervised the building of such a theater himself.

While he had little skill on an instrument, Wagner was a fine conductor, and it was through conducting that he raised some of the money he needed. By the 1870's there were "Wagner Clubs" throughout Germany which also contributed. But the man who above all made possible the spectacular first performance of *The Ring* in its special new theater in Bayreuth in 1876 was King Ludwig II of Bavaria. He spent such fortunes promoting Wagner and his plans that his people were on the
114

Richard Wagner

verge of revolt several times at this misuse of imperial funds.

Wagner's dream of unifying the arts did not succeed. True, the Bayreuth theater was beautiful and functional. The orchestra was put into a pit lower than stage level and the lights were completely dimmed for the first time. Latecomers were not admitted, nor was anything allowed to interfere with the performance. The scenery, costuming, and machinery all contributed to the total theatrical impact of the events on stage. But the music was the most glorious ingredient—far superior to the text and the presentation. Today some opera productions, even at Bayreuth, present his operas on bare stages with modern costuming and lighting, and they are still theatrically effective. Modern audiences recognize that the music, even when performed in concert halls, is the essence of the Wagnerian genius.

What, then, was unique about Wagner's music? Most of all, it was truly continuous sound, wave after wave of sound coming from singers and orchestra together. There were no "arias" artificially separated from the story's dialogue, no "dead spots" for applause or inattention, no choruses dragged on to give the chief singers a rest, no duets unless the story required them. The orchestra was at least equal to, often more important than, the singers themselves. That is why singers had to be specially trained to enlarge their voices, to project them over and yet mingle them with the enormous sound of the large Wagnerian orchestra.

By listening intently to the combined sounds coming from the orchestra and singers, the listener could tell what the characters were thinking and feeling, not merely what they said in song. Wagner accomplished this by means of "leading-motifs," which were short musical "tags" identifying people, places, emotions and objects. For example, there are "motifs" that appear throughout the *Ring* for nature, the Rhine waves, a dwarf, gold, suffering, deceit, youth, a curse, guilt, mockery, love, as well as for each main god and human in the story. In a way, then, the whole story, both in ideas and moods, is told by the orchestra and acted out by the singers.

One critic called the Wagnerian orchestra a "river of

116

sound." The "Wagnerian tubas" were special low brass instruments he had made to emphasize tragic, horrifying or menacing scenes. The endless melodic web was woven by Wagner's skillful use of all the instruments to express every shade of feeling, every ounce of drama. His use of the orchestra was as remarkable as Berlioz's, yet entirely different.

Harmonically, Wagner carried Romanticism to its outer limits, stretching the tonal scales (major and minor) as far as they could be stretched, and using, especially, "chromatic" effects (musical movement by half-steps).

Of all his operas, *Tristan and Isolde,* a searing story of love and sacrifice, was harmonically the most daring. Its harmony created an almost unbearable tension. Wagner's amazing versatility extended also to comic opera. One of his masterpieces is *Die Meistersinger (The Mastersingers of Nurnberg),* a brilliant, five-hour comic opera about the middle ages in which Wagner showed his mastery of polyphony. Religion served as the subject of one of his later operas, *Parsifal.*

Wagner influenced the entire future course of opera, but his impact was even stronger on other fields of music. Hugo Wolf (1860-1903) wrote great songs that were miniature bits of continuous Wagnerian melody divided between singer and piano. Cesar Franck, (1822-1890) the Belgian composer who lived and worked in France, tried to weld Wagnerian chromaticism to the classical forms, succeeding best in his later works such as the *Symphony in D Minor* and the *Symphonic Variations.*

There were three composers who above all owed their musical eminence to their idol, Wagner. One was Anton Bruckner (1824-1896). He tried, not altogether successfully, to fuse the grandiose sounds of Wagner with the symphonic form of Beethoven. A fine organist, he was more successful in his religious polyphonic music.

Gustav Mahler (1860-1911), while worshipping Wagner, was a friend and disciple of Bruckner. One of the greatest of all conductors, in his symphonies he used instrumental colors in original, unexpected ways. His symphonies, enormous in length, incorporated vocal passages and were often based on universal themes of nature, of good and evil, and of resurrection.

Richard Strauss (1864-1949), like Mahler, was a great technician of the orchestra. He used many of Wagner's techniques and added some of his own to write pictorial tone poems. In these he developed his themes to show the psychology of his characters. Among the most inspired and best loved were *Till Eulenspiegel, Death and Transfiguration, Don Juan,* and the autobiographical *A Hero's Life.* While his opera *Salome* caused a scandal by its bizarre subject-matter and treatment, it was his comic opera, *Der Rosenkavalier* (*The Rose Cavalier*) that earned Strauss a permanent place in the world of opera.

Wagner seemed to sweep the whole musical epoch from 1850 on before him. There were, however, pockets of resistance during his lifetime and outright musical rebellion after his death. Arnold Schönberg (1874-1951) could not at first resist Wagner's chromaticism, and in his chamber work *Transfigured Night* outdid Wagner in that technique. He later evolved a new method of composing which was entirely anti-Wagnerian, even anti-romantic. All twelve tones of the octave were treated as absolute equals, with no tone-center as in classical and romantic music. Called the "twelve-tone technique," and heavily mathematical in its method, Schönberg's revolutionary approach had a far-reaching effect on most of the composers of the twentieth century. He also invented a vocal style which was a cross between speech and singing. In his later period, Schönberg began to compose his very brief works such as *Five Pieces for Orchestra.*

One of Schönberg's students, Anton von Webern (1883-1945) carried this concise writing to its extreme. Webern's influence too is strong even today, on both classical and jazz composers. Of all Schönberg's pupils the most imaginative and original was Alban Berg (1885-1935) whose opera *Wozzeck* is one of the greatest of all modern operas, overwhelming in its psychological realism, shattering in its musical and emotional force.

Paul Hindemith (1895-1963) also started out as a Wagnerian romantic, but quite unlike Schönberg in his style. He

118

attempted in his later works to reconcile polyphony with modern rhythms, melodies, and tonal freedom, perhaps most successfully in his opera *Mathis the Painter*. He was one of the most prolific of twentieth century composers, writing extensively in all styles and for all media.

Thus it can be seen that the composers who followed Wagner reacted in various ways to him, positively and negatively. None remained neutral.

claude debussy

1862-1918

If any country would be expected to hold out against Wagner's ideas it was Italy, the birthplace of opera, whose chief export for several centuries was its vocal style and its superb singers. As early as 1817 Gioacchino Rossini (1792-1868), the composer of that great comic opera *The Barber of Seville,* complained that even in Italy "the main melody is strangled in deference to the new German school." Still, Italy, with its gifted melodic opera composers after Rossini, such as Vincenzo Bellini (1801-1835), Gaetano Donizetti (1797-1848), Giuseppe Verdi (1813-1901) and Giacomo Puccini (1858-1924) continued serenely on its way as if Wagner did not exist.

One of the greatest was Verdi, born the same year as Wagner. His strongly dramatic, marvelously melodic operas *Il Trovatore, La Traviata, Aida, Rigoletto* and others are to this day the backbone of opera repertory. There is a story that in composing *Rigoletto* Verdi, at the peak of his success, was afraid to let anyone hear the aria "Woman is Fickle" before the performance. He knew it was so charming and easy to remember that every errand-boy would hum it in the streets, thus making

120

the first performance an anti-climax. He gave it to the tenor to learn only the night before the premiere; it turned out just as he had anticipated.

Verdi was an ardent patriot who was worshipped in Italy as a man as well as the composer of the "hit tunes" of his time. In his very last opera, *Falstaff,* a comic masterpiece written at the age of seventy-nine, Verdi showed his knowledge and respect for Wagner's orchestral techniques. On hearing of Wagner's death he said, "It is a great personality that has disappeared. A name which leaves a mighty imprint upon the history of the art."

The French musical scene was dominated in opera by blaring, spectacular works of Meyerbeer, sentimental works by Charles Gounod (1818-1893), Jules Massenet (1842-1912), and delightful musical comedy-type works by Jacques Offenbach (1819-1880). Little important music other than opera was being written. By 1885 the voice of Wagner began to overcome these weaker French voices.

Where does the Frenchman Claude Debussy fit into all this? Fairly early in life it was obvious that he was no ordinary person. His early childhood was poverty-stricken, rootless and unhappy. As a piano prodigy, he was admitted at ten to the Paris Conservatory and great predictions were made for him as a performer. But he soon showed more interest in composing, and from the start broke every rule, to the despair of his teachers. He was a brilliant student, and won many composition prizes, but always on his musical terms. Shocked but impressed, a teacher once asked him about a certain passage, "What is your rule?" He replied, "My pleasure."

To pursue his musical ideals he made enormous personal sacrifices, living poorly most of his life. He gave piano lessons on his wedding day to scrape together enough to pay for the wedding lunch. He went through crises of self-doubt and desperation, but was lucky enough to have a good friend, the writer Pierre Louys, who managed to pull him through. Claude wrote him, "I really do need your affection, I feel so lonely and helpless . . . I hardly know where I am going if it is not towards suicide . . ." Pierre replied, "You have not the shadow of an

121

excuse for nightmares of this kind, because YOU ARE A GREAT MAN. You must continue with your work, and you must get it known."

Outwardly Debussy was often the life of the party. He frequented cafés with his artist and writer friends, seeking and giving pleasure. He traveled several summers as music teacher with the von Meck family to Russia and other countries of Europe. Madame von Meck (she had been Tchaikovsky's patron) wrote of Debussy, "He enlivens the whole house, he is so very witty and a wonderful mimic."

The first time he visited Bayreuth Debussy fell under the Wagnerian spell. But there was a new, very different, and strong current to artistic and literary thought in Paris in the late 1800's which swept Debussy along with it—Impressionism. Debussy became its musical spokesman, and it is his expansion of music's potential through Impressionism that makes him a heroic figure.

The poets and painters who gathered every evening in cafés or homes to discuss their ideas were bored by the excesses of Romanticism. They rebelled against the emotional extravagance, hysterical outbursts, extreme theatrical effects. Debussy, the only musician in the group, deplored Isolde's "wild screams of frenzy" in Wagner's *Tristan and Isolde*. Impressionism aimed to suggest rather than describe, to show not the detail of an object or situation but rather how it made the artist feel. For the painters, it led to an entirely new form of art, with the main emphasis on design, color and the effects of light rather than the subject. For the poets it meant an appeal to the senses rather than to the mind, with the sound of the words more important than their meaning.

Debussy listened avidly, and arrived at his own conclusions about how all this could be translated into music. He wrote music in which the beat was very subtle, even concealed. He was stimulated not so much by human conflicts as by the ever-changing moods of nature. Yet he did not write the descriptive nature music of Wagner or Richard Strauss. Rather it was a music that evoked the moods of nature as if the listener were experiencing it for the first time. "Music," he wrote, "is the

Giuseppe Verdi

Claude Debussy

expression of the movement of the waters, the play of curves described by changing breezes. There is nothing more musical than a sunset." As a young boy Debussy had hoped to become a sailor. His love of the sea lasted all his life, and inspired some of his greatest works, such as *The Sea, Reflections in the Water, Golden Fish,* and *Sails.* He was able to capture the glittering interplay of sun on sea, the shimmer and haze of wind on water. By the use of wavering chords and delicate handling of the orchestra, by harmonies that seem to melt into each other, he makes us listen from moment to moment, and see water, leaves, wind, clouds, moonlight, snow, with our ears instead of our eyes.

It was his tone poem *Afternoon of a Faun,* based on a poem in the new impressionist form, that marked a turning-point in music history. It told a story, not very clearly or with emphasis, but rather so that the listener is not certain if what happened was real or only a dream. But we sense the mood of the forest and almost feel the leaves fluttering overhead. Vague wisps of melody pour over us lazily, interrupted by bright splashes of sound, leaving uncertain impressions on the listener of sunlight, or perhaps of animals or birds.

Debussy was also the greatest piano composer since Chopin, extending even further the expressive qualities of that instrument. His inspiration for new musical approaches came from many sources. When he heard a Javanese orchestra play for native dancers at the Paris International Exposition he came away with new exotic Oriental scales which he used freely in many compositions. So sensitive was he that a single afternoon spent at a bullfight in Spain gave him enough authentic feel for that country to write such music as *Iberia.*

Debussy's crowning work was his only opera, *Pelléas and Melisande.* In this work he managed to accomplish what Wagner set out to do but never quite achieved. Debussy had once said that he saw the role of a librettist (writer of a play to be used for an opera) as "one who hints at things and will thus enable me to graft my thought on his." What good fortune to find that such a play was already written, and needed only Debussy's musical genius to produce this great opera. But the

124

writing took years. He could not shake off the ghost of Wagner's *Parsifal,* the only one of Wagner's operas he admired.

Maurice Maeterlinck, the Belgian playwright who wrote the play Debussy used, had no feeling for music. "When it comes to music he is like a blind man in a museum," Debussy once said. This made no difference, since Debussy set the play almost word for word, achieving that perfect marriage of word and music for which Wagner strove all his life. So perfectly are the two matched that the music cannot stand alone. Maeterlinck, because of a quarrel with Debussy, vowed he would never see the opera. When he finally did, after Debussy's death, he wrote, "For the first time I have entirely understood my own play."

Here was no conventional opera with sweeping orchestral effects, thunderous loud sounds contrasting with soft, soaring flights of song. Rather it was powerful in a pale sense, creating the tensions of its tragic love story by understatement, by mysterious silences and suggestions of gloom mixed with glimmers of sunshine—a shadowy world of caves and forests. The characters, all too human, were caught up in a web of tragedy. The singing was almost a chant, with the orchestra a quiet mirror of the action. The total effect was almost dreamlike, with one exquisite moment of sound following the other in a gliding, continuous flow.

Debussy lived with his characters for the many years it took to complete the opera, suffering nightmares and tears in the process. At first it aroused violent opposition from both the public and the critics. In it were too many reminders of the strange thoughts buried in our unconscious which dreams bring to light. It was difficult to adjust to music that lacked great climaxes. Eventually *Pelléas and Mélisande* was recognized as one of the great operatic landmarks and Debussy's greatest work.

He continued writing songs, piano music and orchestral works for several more years. By no means were all his works soft, delicate and light. He was at times humorous, brilliant, playful, elegant. His death in 1918 occurred while France was still at war. His country hardly noticed that its greatest musical genius was gone. But his influence was felt everywhere. In

125

England, Frederick Delius (1862-1934) tried to see the English countryside through impressionist eyes; in the United States Charles Griffes (1884-1920) and Charles Loeffler (1875-1937) wrote under his spell; in France itself, his superb use of the harp and the woodwind instruments and his impressionist methods made themselves felt among composers such as Maurice Ravel (1875-1937) and Igor Stravinsky (1882-1971). Under Romanticism music had lost its serenity. Debussy did much to restore it.

igor stravinsky

1882-1971

If Debussy started tremors that shook the foundations of musical Romanticism, Igor Stravinsky was the earthquake that buried it under the shock waves of his genius. No one dreamed that the Russian youngster, brought up in the cold, efficient atmosphere of a busy, wealthy family, would become a rebel. He was brought up correctly, conventionally, and lived that way all his life. It was only in his music that he was unconventional.

His father sang bass in the St. Petersburg Opera. Igor heard much music at home, and was taken to see opera and ballet from his earliest years. He was also thoroughly steeped in the ways of Russian peasant life, which could be violent, morbid, vulgar, barbaric and amusing. He knew their music by listening to it and through the ears of the Russian "Five" composers. It was only after finishing law studies that Igor decided on music as a career. After several years of music study with Rimsky-Korsakov he left for Paris. Ballet attracted him, and Paris was the center of ballet in the early 1900's.

127

Dance had always been important in French music. France had a long history of ballet composers starting even before the days of Jean Lully in the late sixteenth century. What made Paris the goal of every great artist, dancer and composer in the early twentieth century was the presence there of Serge Diaghilev. Diaghilev, director of the Russian Ballet (in Paris) was a genius at recognizing and bringing together many different talents—Picasso and Matisse in the arts, Nijinsky in the ballet and great composers such as Ravel, De Falla, Debussy and Stravinsky, who, at twenty-eight, had not yet made his mark.

Stravinsky's first ballet for Diaghilev, *The Firebird,* produced in 1910, has remained the most popular of all his works—much to Stravinsky's chagrin, since he considered it more Rimskian and Debussian than a display of his own individuality. Debussy said after seeing it, "It haunts me like a beautiful nightmare." Pseudo-Oriental in flavor, it told an old Russian peasant tale. One episode, the Infernal Dance of King Kastchei, had a burning ferocity and originality, and gave a hint of things to come in the way Stravinsky used rhythm as a symbol of power and evil. The instant success of *The Firebird* brought Stravinsky fame overnight.

Petrouchka, produced the next year, showed the tragic life of the poor in Russia under Czarism, with all its misery and persecution. The people, represented by Petrouchka, a sad little sawdust puppet who is nothing more than a toy in the hands of a cruel strong force. By placing the whole action on a puppet stage at a Russian fair, the colorful atmosphere of fun, noise and romance serves as a musical backdrop for the raw and brutal emotions of the puppet's fate. This ballet has Russian folk elements as well as French street tunes, but most remarkable was Stravinsky's handling of the music. One chord often found throughout consisted of both the C and F# major chords used simultaneously. That marked the beginning of the liberation of harmony from the one-key system of Romanticism. "Polytonality," the use of several keys at once, was born. He also used instrumental colors in entirely new ways, and strung small

128

melodic fragments together rather than developing each one in the more traditional way. Audiences were both repelled and fascinated by the new sounds. The vivid, pictorial qualities of the music made *Petrouchka* as well as *The Firebird* stunning concert hall successes that could stand on their own without the presence of dance.

It was his next ballet, *The Rites of Spring*, that made Stravinsky the undisputed leader of twentieth-century music. He himself described its origin this way, "I had a fleeting vision . . . I saw in imagination a solemn pagan rite: sage elders, seated in a circle watching a young girl dance herself to death. They were sacrificing her to the god of spring." His music enacted this brutal, primitive scene so shockingly that it caused a riot at its first performance. Men and women shrieked and screamed. The audience, reacting hysterically, "laughed, spat, hissed, imitated animal cries." The conductor said later, "neighbors began to hit each other over the head with fists or canes . . . soon this anger was concentrated against the orchestra . . . Everything available was tossed in our direction, but we continued to play on . . . Stravinsky had disappeared through a window backstage, to wander dazed along the streets of Paris."

What made this music, much more than the dancing, so extraordinary, so overwhelming, so shattering in its impact? The crude, brutal strength of its melodic line, the nerve-wracking discords, and the amazing new use of percussion instruments helped create a mood of aggression never before expressed in music. But most of all it was the complete emancipation of rhythm from its usual bonds. For the first time rhythms rather than melody or harmony became the central focus of music. The beat was constantly changed, accents shifted, different rhythms pitted against each other, with insistent rhythms hypnotizing the ear. At its premiere in Boston, a local newspaper carried a poem which began:

"Who wrote this fiendish Rite of Spring,
What right had he to write the thing,
Against our helpless ears to fling

Its crash, clash, cling, clang, bing, bang, bing?"

By now these innovations have become commonplace. Yet even today *The Rites of Spring* still retains its extraordinary vitality and excitement.

Stravinsky's shock over that first reception probably helped bring on a very serious illness, to say nothing of a severe emotional crisis. This much is certain—he never wrote in that style again. At first he continued with Russian-based music, ballets and other works, but now instead of writing big sounds for immense orchestras, he went in the opposite direction. He tried to see how economically he could use musical materials, striving for clarity and simplicity. Then he resorted to "Neo-Classicism" (New Classicism). For years he wrote music in the style of various composers he admired, often using actual themes from their works. Sometimes it seemed as if he was mocking certain styles. But all bore the highly individual stamp of the twentieth-century Stravinsky sound. Thus, he wrote a symphony inspired by Bach; a ballet on Pergolesi's music, an opera like one of Tchaikovsky's, a Mozartean opera. In these he showed amazing versatility, craftsmanship, invention. He was exploring the past, flexibly adapting himself to different styles. In the process, however, he lost his popular appeal.

He was very bitter about the fact that his audience "asked him to go backward" to his earlier, popular style. The mass audiences were unable to identify with music utterly lacking in emotional content, which he purged completely from his later works. Yet he continued on his new way with outward calm and self-assurance, turning out many works which were at least respected if not loved. During, and even before, the many years that Stravinsky lived in the United States, he was attracted to jazz, and used jazz rhythms and instrumental ideas in various works such as the *Story of a Soldier,* and *Ragtime for Eleven Instruments.* It was jazz through the Stravinsky filter. He never, however, became a particularly "American" composer.

At the age of seventy he changed course again, beginning to write in the twelve-tone system created many years before by his

130

Igor Stravinsky

great rival in musical circles, Arnold Schönberg. With amazing vitality Stravinsky continued composing for fifteen more years. He also used his keen, orderly mind to collaborate in writing a series of books which expressed his pungent, witty, perceptive opinions on music and on life. The world gave him many honors. He died in 1971 at the age of eighty-eight.

The clue to what he ultimately thought was his greatest contribution to music was his choice of burial place. He had been a French citizen for almost twenty years, and an American citizen for twenty-five. Yet he asked to be buried in Venice near the tomb of the man of whom he once said, "He did his utmost to make the public appreciate me. It gave him real pleasure to produce my work and, indeed, to force it on the more rebellious of my listeners . . . I have a sense of gratitude, deep attachment and admiration for him . . ." That man was Serge Diaghilev.

His earliest works were probably his best. In the fifty years since *The Rites of Spring,* three generations of composers have been influenced by Stravinsky. He had a decisive effect on many concert composers such as Serge Prokofieff (1891-1953) and Mexico's Carlos Chavez. Much of the jazz, popular, television and movie music heard today would sound very different if Stravinsky had not composed. He was indeed a giant among composers.

two american heroes

America's folk music goes back to its earliest days, but its composed music of originality started with the twentieth-century. True, there were early amateur composers—William Billings (1746-1800) in colonial days wrote tunes for use in Puritan churches. Stephen Foster (1826-1864), almost an amateur, intrigued by popular entertainments such as the minstrel show, wrote the sentimental songs, *Oh, Susannah* and *Old Folks at Home*. Louis Gottschalk (1829-1869) captured some of the captivating rhythms of Caribbean and Creole folk songs in his music for piano. But most serious American composers went to Germany to study and then came home to write pale imitations of Mendelssohn and Brahms.

Not until the beginning of the twentieth century did the first authentic American musical hero, a Connecticut Yankee named Charles Ives (1874-1954) appear on the scene. His father was a bandmaster, a thoroughly trained musician who also had the greatest curiosity about sounds in general. He conducted imaginative sound experiments with the eager participation of his son. To see what happened when sounds collided with each other he once stationed three bands in different parts of town and had them cross each other, playing different music in different rhythms. He passed on to Charles not only a complete background of the European musical tradition and familiarity with its music and its instruments, but also a joyous sense of musical adventure and exploration.

Among his early experiences Charles listened to band

rehearsals, rhythmic country fiddling at barn dances, hymn singing in church, songs by his father's friend Stephen Foster, theater and minstrel shows, college songs, outdoor religious camp-meeting services at which thousands sang, and great chamber music classics played at home by his father and friends. He loved the national holidays, and knew the army bugle calls and patriotic songs, including those of the North and South from the Civil War. He especially loved football and baseball. He had begun to write music when he was eleven, and by thirteen he held a regular job as organist in a local church. When people became excited about his early compositions and asked him what he played he would reply gruffly, "shortstop."

His music composition teachers at Yale University refused to take his work seriously. It was full of broken rules but was original, sometimes eccentric, and always had fresh and powerful ideas. While at college he listened to pianists in the local taverns play ragtime (an early form of jazz) and sometimes played it himself in nearby bars and theaters. For several years in college and afterwards he supported himself as a church organist.

Some early experiences with professional musicians who ridiculed what he wrote as unplayable did not stop his fierce independence. "I am the only one who likes any of my music," he once said. His father died while he was still a freshman at college, but his influence never ended. "Father felt that a man could keep his music interest stronger, cleaner, bigger and freer if he didn't try to make a living out of it." Ives decided to make his living through selling insurance. With a partner, he built an insurance agency that eventually did $450 million in sales. He wrote manuals on insurance that are still in use. As a composer he went "underground," composing secretly every day after work, weekends and holidays, with the complete support of his wife, whose name was, appropriately, Harmony.

By day he used his keen mind to solve knotty business problems. He did not attend concerts, listen to music, or have contact with other musicians. He performed a second day's work every night in front of his music desk, tossing each completed

134

composition into a drawer. In the twenty years between 1900 and 1920 he wrote as much as a composer might reasonably expect to write in a lifetime, working full time. Ives did all this without the slightest encouragement from the public or publishers, or even the opportunity to hear any of his works performed. Later he said, "You cannot set an art off in the corner and hope for it to have vitality, reality and substance . . . It comes directly out of the heart of experience of life and thinking about life and living life. My work in music helped my business and the work in business helped my music."

What does his music sound like? He makes listeners stretch their ears because of his complete break with the European mainstream of music, which he said was "drugged with an overdose of habit-forming sounds." Both simple and complex at the same time, his music is utterly American, evoking American life around the turn of the century. It is by turns harsh on the ears, satirical, gay or haunting. Never is it sweet or sentimental. Ives did not hesitate to mix parts of Beethoven, Dvorak or Tchaikovsky with any of the American music—religious, patriotic, country or ragtime that he had ever heard. All forms of music were equally good, in his judgment, if they contributed to the musical ideas he wanted to express.

In his search for new kinds of musical expression he showed true genius, anticipating the musical innovations of the most far-out composers yet to come, in Europe and America. He hit on polytonality and irregular rhythm structures twenty years before the *Rites of Spring*. His *Fourth Symphony* at times has as many as seventeen different rhythms going on at once. He used atonality long before Schönberg, Bartokian discords before Bartok, also tone clusters and quarter tones. "Chance" music, in which players are given only guidelines rather than actual notes to play within a given time span, was "invented" officially in the 1960's. But thirty years before Ives had indicated, "from here on the bassoon may play anything at will."

He suffered a severe physical breakdown after World War I (perhaps brought on by the war itself, which shocked him out of his healthy, optimistic, positive attitude towards men and life).

135

Practically speaking, his creative life was over when he was about forty-five, although he died at eighty. It was gradually, during the latter years, that his works began to be published and known. At first Ives published them himself, giving away free copies to anyone who asked for them. Even later, he refused to make any money out of his music, turning any fees or royalties he received into scholarships and other aid for young composers, especially those he felt were as experimental, daring and bold as he had been.

Musicians struggled over the impossibilities of his scores and eventually found them to be possible. Critics as well as audience began to realize there was a genius in their midst. The earlier antagonism and hilarity were replaced by reviews which said "imagination and a strange genius . . . an audacious talent . . . at times awkward and raw, but there is real power and true invention . . . his art is truly national. The new headlines read "Tardy Recognition" . . . "Charles Ives at Last." He was awarded the Pulitzer Prize in 1947 for his *Third Symphony* (written more than forty years before). To the very end he could not quite believe in his success, and refused to attend any performance of his works. Today there is scarcely a major orchestra that has not played his *Holidays Symphony, Three Places in New England,* and *The Unanswered Question.* Pianists spend years studying his *Concord Sonata,* and his songs appear increasingly at song recitals.

Charles Ives was not very self-critical, and his work shows signs of haste, but he was undoubtedly an authentic musical hero. Yet no one turns off the record-player humming his melodies—he was not that kind of composer. But our next hero was. His name was George Gershwin (1898-1937).

Unlike the steady childhood of Ives, George's struggling, warm-hearted family moved almost thirty times to various apartments in New York City, where he lived his short life. He was a typical city boy, scrappy, enjoying street games, and an average student. At twelve he started piano lessons, and it was soon obvious that only popular songs interested him. From his earliest teens he was fascinated with Negro music, ragtime and blues, which he heard when his family lived in Harlem.

136

Charles Ives

George Gershwin

By fifteen he quit school to take a $15-a-week job as a "song-plugger" for a music publishing company. For eight or ten hours a day he pounded a piano in a tiny room for vaudeville and later, radio performers who shopped the publishing houses for new material. At twenty-one, having already written a musical comedy, George composed his first big hit, *Swanee*, which sold millions of copies. During the remaining eighteen years of his life (he died at 39) George wrote over seven hundred songs and more than twenty-five musical comedies which were produced on Broadway, as well as music for films. His songs were far superior to the songs of the day; they had enchanting melodies, infectious rhythms, wistful charm and sparkling vitality. Almost all were written to words by George's older brother, Ira. George and Ira were one of those made-in-heaven partnerships in words and music, like Rodgers and Hammerstein many years later. Among the many Gershwin songs that are still known, played and loved throughout the world are, *I Got Rhythm, The Man I Love, Embraceable You, Somebody Loves You, Lady Be Good,* and *A Foggy Day.* But his "heroism" stemmed from an idea he once expressed, "Jazz I regard as an American folk music . . . I believe that it can be made the basis of serious symphonic works of lasting value . . . Jazz is the result of the energy stored up in America. It is a very energetic kind of music, noisy, boisterous, and even vulgar . . . It will leave its mark on future music."

When the conductor Paul Whiteman asked George to write a symphonic work that would use the jazz idiom, he started a musical revolution as significant as Stravinsky's *Rites of Spring*. George did not have enough technical skill to do the arrangement for orchestra himself, but that did not prevent the *Rhapsody in Blue* from becoming, on its first performance in 1924, a milestone in musical history. It was music of the city, sophisticated but also naive, nervous, restless, yet "blues-y." By the time he wrote *An American in Paris* and the *Piano Concerto,* George had acquired the technique to write for the orchestra himself. Through these works he made jazz "respectable," bringing it into the concert hall. This led dozens of composers to

138

follow his example, although seldom as successfully. At the same time he alerted popular composers to the possibility of wedding classical techniques to their materials. If popular, jazz and rock music today draw freely from both fields, it is due in large part to Gershwin's example.

A remarkable jazz pianist, Gershwin brought a new freedom to improvising at the piano. The director at the premiere of *Porgy and Bess* wrote, "He would draw a lovely melody out of the keyboard like a golden thread, then he would play with it and juggle it, twist it and toss it around mischievously, weave it into unexpected intricate patterns, tie it in knots and untie it, and hurl it into a cascade of ever-changing rhythms." He had a dynamic, magnetic personality, and spent most of his waking hours composing or playing, surrounded by admiring friends and musicians in the frenzied, hectic atmosphere of New York in the twenties and thirties.

Gershwin's greatest achievement came near the end of his life, when he wrote the first significant American folk-opera, *Porgy and Bess.* Already steeped in urban Negro blues and jazz, he stayed for some time in an isolated southern Negro community (the setting of the opera) to absorb the deeper, older roots of spirituals, "shouts" and street-calls. It was a landmark work in many ways, in addition to the brilliance of its music. It was the first opera to use an almost completely Negro cast, thus starting many black singers on their careers. It forced the National Theater in Washington, D.C. to desegregate. The opera became the State Department's most popular cultural export to countries throughout the world. The very original score included such wonderful songs as *Summertime* and *It Ain't Necessarily So,* choral chants, sweet melodies, and dramatic passages based on Negro chants and spirituals. The recitatives (half-spoken passages) were grounded in Negro speech. In all, *Porgy and Bess* brought the Negro roots and musical richness of jazz and blues to the surface. It helped white audiences appreciate those idioms, thus enlarging opportunities for black performers and black music in this country and abroad.

World War II enriched American music by a wave of

European composers (as well as performers) who sought refuge, voluntarily exiling themselves from the horrors of Europe at that time. From among these, as well as native-born composers, white and black, there have been many fine American composers in addition to Ives and Gershwin. They have worked in every style—neo-romantic, neo-classic, atonal, electronic, and "chance." There are exciting young composer-performers in rock and jazz music today. But it is too soon to tell which of them are doing work of such significance that it will change the direction of music's history.

What about heroines? There have been great women performers, as singers, violinists, pianists. And there have been women composers as far back as Monteverdi's time and before. But none of them has as yet reached the musical heights of the composer-heroes that have been the subject of this book. The reason remains a mystery. Perhaps in the past not enough women had the opportunity for the needed intensive musical education. Perhaps composing was not considered a "lady-like" occupation when women began working outside of the home. Perhaps the world of the concert and opera house, so long (and still) dominated by men, did not give women composers enough chance to be heard. But times and attitudes are changing. There are women writing fine music today in all styles, including electronic and popular music. Perhaps now, somewhere among them, or still growing up, is the woman who will one day be recognized as a "heroine" of music.

glossary of instruments

The following is a partial list of the instruments usually found in symphony orchestras, military and brass bands, and jazz and rock groups, plus several of the most common solo and folk instruments. First the families of instruments are described. Each instrument, plus many more, can be found separately defined in the alphabetical listing which follows the "families" discussion.

■ STRING FAMILY

The sounds are produced by the vibration of strings which are "stopped" by the fingers to get the right length for the desired pitch. The vibrations are made either by plucking the string by hand or pick or by drawing a horsehair bow across it. The orchestral instruments played with a bow are (from highest range of sound to lowest) the *violin, viola, cello* and *double bass.* The string instrument that is always played by plucking is the

141

harp. In a full symphony orchestra of about 110 players, as many as seventy-five may be string players.

■ WOODWIND FAMILY
(often made today of metal or plastic)

These are basically tubes, with holes, that enclose a column of air. The length of the column is changed by covering the holes with fingers. In the *flute* and *piccolo,* the air is blown across a mouth-opening into the tube; in the *recorder* the air is blown directly into a mouthpiece; in the *clarinet* and *saxophone* a single reed is vibrated by the action of the tongue against a mouthpiece; the *oboe, English horn* and *bassoon* do the same with a double reed. All the above instruments are found in the symphony orchestra except the recorder, which is a small-ensemble or solo instrument, and the saxophone, which is used in bands and jazz groups. In a full symphony orchestra of about 110 players, about sixteen may be woodwind players.

■ BRASS FAMILY

These are tubes in which the air is vibrated by being blown into directly through a cup- or funnel-shaped mouthpiece. Those usually found in a symphony orchestra (from the highest range of sound to the lowest) are the *trumpet, horn* (also known as French horn), *trombone* and *tuba.* The horn, trumpet and tuba have valves which, when pressed, change the length of the tubing and therefore the pitch. The trombone simply slides its tubing in or out to change its length. At every tube length, on all these instruments, several different notes can be produced by tightening or loosening the lip tension against the mouthpieces.

In bands there are also frequently found the mellophone (related to the horn), the cornet and the flügelhorn (related to the

142

trumpet), and the baritone, euphonium and Sousaphone (all related to the tuba). In a full symphony orchestra of 110 players, about thirteen may be brass players.

■ PERCUSSION FAMILY

These instruments usually produce their sounds by being struck or shaken. Some, such as the *bass drum, snare drum, timpani* and *tambourine* have surfaces made of stretched skins. Others, such as the *celesta, chimes, xylophone* and *glockenspiel,* have plates or bars arranged like keyboards, with resonating surfaces of wood or metal. There are others such as *cymbals, gong* and *triangle* which are used for special effects. Since only a few of these instruments are ever used at once, there are usually no more than four or five percussion players in a full symphony orchestra of 110.

■ VIOL FAMILY

These were bowed string instruments widely used in the sixteenth through eighteenth centuries. They came in several sizes, one being known as the viola da gamba (leg viol). Another was the viola d'amore, which had a second set of strings under the ones played on, giving a special kind of resonance. The only descendants of the viols that are still in common use today are the bass viol, now called the *double bass,* and the violoncello, often called simply *cello.*

■ ELECTRONIC INSTRUMENTS

Some of these, like the electric guitar, are only amplified (the sound enlarged) by electronic means. True electronic instruments are those which produce the original sound electronically. There are some electronic organs and electronic bells. Also, tape recorders are used to create new sounds by changing recording speeds. Sometimes existing sounds are merged together by tape, so that the tape recorder is itself the source of the final sound.

Some electronic instruments such as the synthesizer are actually computers. They can be programmed to produce sounds of particular pitches and qualities. They can be made to imitate the sounds of human voices or existing instruments. They can also produce new sounds by the electronic manipulation of sound waves.

While they are not usually found in the standard symphony orchestra, band or jazz group, electronic instruments are coming into increasing popularity both as solo instruments and in combination with existing instruments and voices.

ALPHABETICAL LISTING OF INSTRUMENTS

Bass Drum: A percussion instrument consisting of a large wooden cylinder, having both sides covered with tightly stretched skin and played with a stick having a large felt-covered knob, or sometimes with regular drumsticks. It has a very deep, booming sound and is used in symphony orchestras, bands and jazz groups.

Bassoon: A woodwind instrument of the oboe family (double reed), consisting of a long wooden pipe doubled back on itself. It has a wide range and rich quality but can also

144

produce a rough, buzzing awkward sound (for comic effects). The double bassoon has the same shape but is larger. It has the lowest range of all the woodwind instruments. Both bassoon and double bassoon are used in symphony orchestras and bands.

Celesta: A percussion instrument that has a keyboard and is played like a piano. The keys strike a set of tuned metal plates in a resonating box, producing a very delicate, bell-like sound. It is used in symphony orchestras.

Cello (short for *violoncello*): Shaped like a violin, but over twice as long and broad. One of the bowed string instruments, it is rested on the floor and held between the knees of the player. The right hand draws the bow across strings that have been "stopped" to the desired length by the left-hand fingers. The tone can be deep and powerful, but also rich and velvety. It has a large range, and is used in symphony orchestras and occasionally in jazz groups.

Clarinet: A single reed instrument having the largest range of all the woodwind instruments. It is very versatile, with sounds rich and full in its lower range, bright and brilliant in the upper. There are various sizes including bass clarinet and soprano clarinet (the latter used most often in bands). It is found in symphony orchestras, bands and jazz groups.

Clavichord: One of the forerunners of the piano, this oblong-shaped keyboard instrument was particularly popular in the sixteenth century. When a key is pressed, a piece of brass strikes a string producing a soft and delicate tone. It is only usable in small rooms as a solo instrument or amplified for recording or broadcasting.

Cymbals: A percussion instrument consisting of two large brass plates which are struck together. It is used in orchestras and bands. In jazz groups, a single cymbal is held on a frame, attached to a bass drum and hit with a drum stick. The two together produce a loud, metallic crashing sound; the single one produces a sound like a gong.

Double bass (also called bass *viol* or simply *bass*): Largest of the bowed string instruments, it is tall enough to be played

145

standing up. Its tone is deep and heavy; it is used in symphony orchestras and jazz groups. In the latter, it is almost always played by plucking. It appears occasionally in bands.

Drum (side and snare drums, etc.): A percussion instrument, usually a wood or metal cylinder with skin stretched tightly over one or both sides. Much smaller than the bass drum, it is played by striking the drum head with a stick or sticks. It is capable of very fast and intricate rhythmic patterns. "Snares" are detachable strings of gut or wire stretched over the lower head of a drum. They give a rattling effect when the player strikes the upper head with drumsticks. Used in symphony orchestras, bands and jazz groups. Latin-American drums such as the bongo and samba drums are usually struck with the hands.

English horn: A double reed member of the woodwind section, it is actually a slightly larger, deeper-voiced oboe. Its tone is more mellow and melancholy than the oboe. It is used in symphony orchestras and bands.

Flute: One of the woodwind instruments which has a wide range. Its lower notes are breathy and velvety, its higher notes are sweet, but it can also be bright and penetrating. It is held horizontally and used in symphony orchestras and bands. It is also frequently used by some jazz groups.

Glockenspiel (chime-playing): A percussion instrument made of metal bars of different lengths attached to a frame. Played by striking with a hard rubber mallet, it has a high, tinkling tone. It is used in symphony orchestras and bands.

Gong: A percussion instrument consisting of a large brass plate (four to five feet across) suspended on a rack. Played by lightly striking with a beater, it has a deep, mysterious, muffled sound; when struck hard, a crashing, resounding sound. It is used in symphony orchestras.

Guitar: A string instrument with a fretted fingerboard (notes separated by metal bars). It is played by plucking with the fingers or strumming with a pick. There are several varieties: the classical guitar, Hawaiian guitar and steel guitar. The classical guitar is widely used as a solo instrument. The steel

146

guitar, amplified, is used by jazz and rock groups. Other popular fretted folk instruments are the banjo and the ukulele.

Harp: The only plucked string instrument in the orchestra. It consists of forty-seven strings and seven pedals which serve to change the pitch of the strings. It is large and triangle-shaped and rests on the floor. The harp is held upright and is plucked by four fingers of each hand. The sound is soft and silvery, yet capable of brilliant, sweeping effects. It is used mainly in symphony orchestras, however, there are several jazz harpists.

Harpsichord: One of the piano's ancestors, having a keyboard instrument resembling a small grand piano. In place of the clavichord's hammers, the strings are plucked by strips of leather or goose quills when a key is pressed. Its tone is stronger than the clavichord's and more delicate than the piano's. As a solo instrument, it is used mostly for music written during the sixteenth to eighteenth centuries. It is also used occasionally by jazz groups.

Horn (sometimes called "French horn"): It has the greatest range of all the brass instruments with its tubing curled into a round shape and the mouthpiece funnel-shaped. The quality and pitch of the tone can be changed by inserting a hand in the bell of the instrument (called "muting"). Its beautiful mellow tone can also sound muffled, mysterious, or brilliantly clear. Valves when depressed by fingers can change the tube's length. Additional pitch changes are made by changing the lip tension. It is used in symphony orchestras and bands. The mellophone, similar to the horn, is another band instrument.

Kettledrum: (see *Timpani*)

Oboe: A double-reed instrument of the woodwind family with a penetrating, nasal, almost mournful tone. It is usually used for pastoral, plaintive or Oriental effects, in symphony orchestras and bands.

Organ: A keyboard wind instrument. In a pipe organ, the sound is produced by air blown through pipes by means of bellows. The pipes are operated by pressing keys on one or more keyboards plus a pedal board operated by the feet.

In electric organs, an electronic source supplies air to the pipes. A solo instrument of great power, with penetrating tone, it is capable of great variations of loudness and quality of tone. The pipe organ is usually found in churches and, occasionally, in homes. Electronic organs are used in homes and by jazz and rock groups.

Piano (short for *pianoforte,* meaning "loud-soft"):   The piano was the first keyboard instrument that could produce gradations of tone by lighter or stronger touch. It was also the first keyboard instrument with pedals which could sustain tones. Each "string" is a group of two or three strings. When key is depressed a damper (small felt-covered piece of wood) is lifted from the string, allowing it to vibrate. By pressing the damper pedal, causing all the dampers to be raised, it allows all the depressed keys to continue sounding.

The sounding board, a flat sheet of wood, magnifies the sound. There are other pedals that make soft sounds possible, and enable the player to sustain only particular notes played. The piano can be considered either a string or a percussion instrument. A solo instrument blending extremely well with other instruments and voices, it is a regular member only of jazz groups.

Piccolo (meaning "small"):   The piccolo is the smallest orchestral instrument and the highest pitched of the woodwinds. It is held horizontally as the flute, but is half its size. It has a brilliant, bright tone, piercing in its higher register. It is found in symphony orchestras and bands.

Recorder: An early instrument of the flute type, it is held vertically, and blown directly into the mouthpiece. It was most popular from the Middle Ages to eighteenth century, and is currently enjoying revival. There are several different sizes. It has a sweet, pleasing tone and is popular for school and home use.

Saxophone: The saxophone belongs to a family of instruments invented in 1846. A single-reed metal instrument (resem-

148

bling the clarinet), with a penetrating, sweet, mellow, brilliant, rough, or "edgy" tone. It is used primarily by bands and jazz groups.

Tambourine: This hand-held percussion instrument consists of a small single-headed drum mounted on one side of a shallow, circular wooden hoop. Small loose metal disks called jingles are set into the wood. It may be tapped with fingers or shaken. It has a penetrating single rap-jingle of sound or a steady roll. Usually used by symphony orchestras, bands, and jazz groups.

Timpani (also called *Kettledrums*): The timpani has a parchment-like skin stretched over the opening of a large copper bowl and can produce a definite pitch. Handles or pedals are used to change tension of the drum head, thus changing pitch as required. There are usually three in an orchestra, all played with covered drumsticks. Its tone ranges from delicate and soft to very loud; it is is used only in symphony orchestras.

Triangle: A small percussion instrument made of a round steel rod bent into a triangular shape. It is played by being struck with a small steel rod and has a tinkling, penetrating sound. It is used in symphony orchestras and bands.

Trombone: A brass instrument with a cup mouthpiece. The player moves a slide back and forth to change basic pitches. Additional pitch changes are made by changing lip tension. Although there are various sizes, the tenor trombone is most popular. Its tone is deep and powerful, but can also be majestic, solemn, lyrical or humorous. It is used in symphony orchestras, bands and jazz groups.

Trumpet: A brass instrument with a cup mouthpiece, it is the highest-pitched of the brasses. Valves can be depressed by fingers to change tube length. Additional pitch changes are made by changing lip tension. It has a penetrating, brilliant tone quality and is found in symphony orchestras, bands and jazz groups.

Tuba: It is the lowest-pitched brass instrument, with a cup mouthpiece. Valves are depressed by fingers to change tube length. Additional changes of pitch are made by changing lip tension. The tone is deep and rumbling, sometimes gruff, occasionally it is used humorously. It is found in symphony orchestras. Bands and jazz groups often use related instruments such as the baritone, euphonium and Sousaphone.

Viola: A bowed string instrument, slightly larger than the violin. It is held under the chin. The right hand draws the bow across strings that have been "stopped" to the desired length by the left-hand fingers. The tone is slightly veiled—less brilliant than the violin, but somewhat mellow and sad. It is used in symphony orchestras.

Violin: The violin is the smallest of the bowed string instruments. It is held under the chin. The right hand draws the bow across strings that have been "stopped" to the desired length by the left-hand fingers. It has a great variety of tone—brilliant, singing, vigorous, tender, or ghostly. The violin is the most versatile and numerous of all orchestral instruments. It is used in symphony orchestras, occasionally in jazz bands, and often as a folk instrument ("fiddle") in country music.

Xylophone: A percussion instrument of definite pitch, consisting of two rows of wooden bars of varying lengths, arranged like a piano keyboard. There are metal resonators anchored underneath. It is played with mallets, producing a hard "wooden" clattering sound and used in symphony orchestras, bands and jazz groups. A related instrument, the vibraphone, which has metal bars and a sustaining pedal, is found in jazz groups.

selected bibliography

Arnold, Denis, *Monteverdi*, Farrar, Straus and Cudahy, New York: 1963.

Bauer, Marion and Ethel Peyser, *Music through the Ages*, Putnam, New York: 1967.

Brown, Maurice J. E., *Schubert: A Critical Biography*, St. Martin's, New York: 1958.

Burk, John, *The Life and Works of Beethoven*, Modern Library, New York: 1943.

Chase, Gilbert, *America's Music from the Pilgrims to the Present*, McGraw Hill, New York: 1966.

David, Hans T. and Arthur Mendel, eds., *The Bach Reader: A Life of Johann Sebastian Bach in Letters and Documents*, Norton, New York: 1966.

Donington, Robert, *The Instruments of Music*, Methuen, London: 1970.

Ewen, David, *Journey to Greatness: The Life and Music of George Gershwin*, Prentice-Hall, Englewood Cliffs: 1970.

Finkelstein, Sidney, *Composer and Nation: The Folk Heritage of Music*, International Publishers, New York: 1960.

Fischer, Hans Conrad and Lutz Beach, *The Life of Mozart*, St. Martin's, New York: 1969.

Geiringer, Karl, *Brahms: His Life and Works*, Allen and Unwin, London: 1948.

Howard, John Tasker, *Stephen Foster, America's Troubadour*, Crowell, New York: 1953.

Hughes, Rupert, *Music Lovers' Encyclopedia*, Deems Taylor and Russell Kerr, eds., Garden City Books, Garden City: 1954.

151

Jacob, H. E., *Joseph Haydn: His Art, Times and Glory,* Richard and Clara Winston, trs., Rinehart, New York: 1950.

Jacobs, Arthur, *A New Dictionary of Music,* Aldine, Chicago: 1961.

Jacobs, Robert L., *Wagner,* Farrar, Straus & Giroux, New York: 1965.

Jones, L., *Blues People: Negro Music in White America,* Morrow, New York: 1963.

Keepnews, Orrin and Bill Grauer, Jr., *A Pictorial History of Jazz,* Crown, New York: 1955.

Lang, Paul Henry, *George Frideric Handel,* Norton, New York: 1966.

...................., and Otto Bettmann, *A Pictorial History of Music,* Norton, New York: 1960.

Malone, Bill C., *Country Music, U.S.A: A Fifty-Year History,* University of Texas Press, Austin: 1968.

Maynard, Olga, *Enjoying Opera: A Book for the New Opera Goer,* Scribner, New York: 1966.

Rimsky-Korsakoff, Nikolay, *My Musical Life,* Judah A. Joffe, tr., Knopf, New York: 1923.

Seroff, Victor, *Franz Liszt,* Books for Libraries Press, Freeport: 1966.

...................., *Hector Berlioz,* Macmillan, New York: 1967.

Siohan, Robert, *Stravinsky,* Eric Walter White, tr., Grossman, New York: 1970.

Thompson, Oscar, *Debussy, Man and Artist,* Dover, New York: 1967.

Valentin, Erich, *Beethoven: A Pictorial Biography,* Thames and Hudson, London: 1958.

Weinstock, Herbert, *Chopin: The Man and His Music,* Knopf, New York: 1965.

Young, Percy M., *Tragic Muse: The Life and Works of Robert Schumann,* Dobson, London: 1961.

...................., *Tchaikovsky,* David White, New York: 1968.

index

index

155

156